Would You Believe . . . ?

- The first animated cartoon character in history was a dinosaur.

- When the film *The Lost World* was released in 1925, many people thought the dinosaurs in it were real.

- The original plan for *King Kong* called for Kong to be played by a real gorilla, and the dinosaurs to be played by real lizards.

- Godzilla became so popular in the U.S. that he had his own TV show, "The Godzilla Power Hour."

Find out many more wild and amazing facts in this book about your favorite dinosaur heroes and villains!

Books by Daniel Cohen

GHOSTLY TERRORS
THE GREATEST MONSTERS IN THE WORLD
HOLLYWOOD DINOSAUR
HORROR IN THE MOVIES
THE MONSTERS OF STAR TREK
MONSTERS YOU NEVER HEARD OF
REAL GHOSTS
THE RESTLESS DEAD
SCIENCE FICTION'S GREATEST MONSTERS
STRANGE AND AMAZING FACTS ABOUT STAR TREK
SUPERMONSTERS
THE WORLD'S MOST FAMOUS GHOSTS

Books by Daniel and Susan Cohen

HEROES OF THE CHALLENGER
THE KID'S GUIDE TO HOME COMPUTERS
ROCK VIDEO SUPERSTARS
ROCK VIDEO SUPERSTARS II
WRESTLING SUPERSTARS
WRESTLING SUPERSTARS II
YOUNG AND FAMOUS: HOLLYWOOD'S NEWEST
  SUPERSTARS
YOUNG AND FAMOUS: SPORTS' NEWEST
  SUPERSTARS

Available from ARCHWAY paperbacks

HOLLYWOOD DINOSAUR

DANIEL COHEN

AN ARCHWAY PAPERBACK
Published by POCKET BOOKS • NEW YORK

Illustrations are used by permission and through the courtesy of:
Lippert, 1951: viii; *Illustrated London News:* 3; NYPL Picture
Collection: 5, 6; Jerry Ohlinger's Movie Material: 13, 14, 17, 86, 98–
99, 115; RKO, 1933: 23, 24, 25; Allied Artists, 1959: 26; © 1953
Warner Bros., All Rights Reserved: 32–33; Toho, 1954: 40; Toho,
1965: 45; Toho, 1969: 47; Hal Roach Studios, Inc., *One Million B.C.*,
© 1940, renewed 1967, © 1987: 56, 58–59; Hammer Films, 1966: 65,
66–67; © 1969 Warner Bros. –7 Arts, All Rights Reserved: 71; ©
1954 Warner Bros., All Rights Reserved: 73; © 1959 Joseph M.
Schenck Enterprises, Inc., and Twentieth Century–Fox Film Corp.,
All Rights Reserved: 78–79; Amicus/American International, 1976:
80–81; Amicus/American International, 1974: 83; © The Walt Disney Company: 89; © 1985 Touchstone Films: 92; Columbia Pictures,
1957: 106

AN ARCHWAY PAPERBACK *Original*

An Archway Paperback published by
POCKET BOOKS, a division of Simon & Schuster, Inc.
1230 Avenue of the Americas, New York, N.Y. 10020

ISBN: 0-671-64598-6

First Archway Paperback printing December 1987

10 9 8 7 6 5 4 3 2 1

AN ARCHWAY PAPERBACK and colophon are
registered trademarks of Simon & Schuster, Inc.

Printed in the U.S.A.

IL 4+

CONTENTS

HOLLYWOOD
DINOSAUR

Publicity photo from a low-budget 1951 dinosaur epic, *The Lost Continent*. With dinosaurs battling overhead, what could our heroes possibly be staring at?

1

EARLY FAME

On Hollywood Boulevard, in front of what used to be the gaudy Grauman's Chinese Theater, there is an area on the sidewalk where film stars would come and put their footprints, or handprints in wet cement. At one time all the big Hollywood films had their world premieres at Grauman's Chinese Theater. Grauman's is not what it used to be. Even Hollywood Boulevard is no longer a chic nor glamorous street. But the footprints of the stars are still there, and tourists still come from all over the world to see them.

You'll find the footprints of Charlie Chaplin, Marilyn Monroe, Humphrey Bogart—nearly all the great stars. But you won't find any dinosaur footprints—which is really a shame. There should be an extra large slab of cement set aside for a gigantic dinosaur footprint. It's only fitting. It's only fair. Because dinosaurs have been among the biggest—in both senses of that word—stars that Hollywood has ever had. As they might say in Hollywood, dinosaurs have been boffo box office, since films began. Since before films began.

Dinosaurs have been big show biz attractions from the time people discovered that there were such things as dinosaurs. About 175 years ago scientists first began to realize that some very, very large, and very strange looking creatures lived on earth a long time ago. The word *dinosaur* was coined by the British scientist Sir Richard Owen. It means "terrible lizard" in Latin. It's not really a proper name. Dinosaurs are not just big lizards. Many of them were peace-loving plant eaters who were not terrible at all. But the name has stuck.

It first became apparent just how boffo dinosaurs were going to be in show biz, way back in 1852. In the previous year there was the Great Exhibition, a sort of World's Fair, held in London. The centerpiece for the Great Exhibition was called the Crystal Palace—the largest glass and iron building ever constructed. The Great Exhibition was a great success. When the Exhibition closed the promoters thought it would be a shame just to destroy the beautiful Crystal Palace. Instead the building was taken apart and moved from the center of London to what was then a suburban park. There it was to

Before putting his dinosaur models on display at the Crystal Palace, sculptor Waterhouse Hawkins held a dinner for some of England's leading scientists—inside his model of the iguanodon.

be reconstructed and used as a museum for the arts and sciences.

The developers, however, were worried. They were afraid that people wouldn't go all the way out to the suburbs even to see the famous Crystal Palace.

The new museum needed something extra, something sensational, to bring out the crowds. Queen Victoria's husband Prince Albert had been one of the sponsors of the Great Exhibition. He got the idea of putting reconstructions of prehistoric animals, including dinosaurs, around the Crystal Palace. He figured the reconstructions would be educational and just sensational enough to attract the paying customers.

The models were to be made by a famous sculptor named Waterhouse Hawkins. The construction of the dinosaur models was to be supervised by the man who named them—the scientist Richard Owen.

From a scientific point of view the models constructed by Hawkins and Owen were absolutely awful. The scientist and the sculptor only had fragmentary remains to work with, so they could only guess what the whole dinosaur looked like. Most of the time they guessed wrong.

For example, we now know that the iguanodon walked upright on two powerful hind legs.

Two reconstructions of the iguanodon: the early incorrect version and the more nearly correct upright
version.

Nineteenth-century drawings of dinosaurs were usually inaccurate, and almost always showed the beasts locked in a death struggle.

But the Hawkins-Owen model makes it look like a cross between a lizard and a rhinoceros. It was a scaly, heavy-bodied creature that stood squarely on four stumpy legs. The creature even has a "horn" on its nose. Later it was discovered the "horn" was really a thumb joint.

In the years that followed, a lot of scientists criticized and ridiculed the models. But that didn't matter one little bit to the public. When the models were put on view in 1853 huge crowds turned out to gape and gawk at these astonishing creatures called dinosaurs. In fact, the public still turns out to look at them. The Crystal Palace itself burned down in 1936. But the dinosaur models are still there in the park. And people still come to gape and gawk.

Even before the dinosaur models were made for the Crystal Palace there were some popular books on dinosaurs. The pictures usually showed dinosaurs in a death struggle, grabbing one another by the throat and rolling on the ground. The books were very sensational, and very popular.

By the 1870s a large number of dinosaur fossils were being unearthed, particularly in the United States. Whole dinosaur skeletons could be reconstructed. Sometimes a showman would get possession of one of these skeletons and tour the country with it. People would pay as much as a dime, a lot of money in those days, just for the chance to look at one of the huge skeletons.

Most of the fossils, however, went to museums. When they were put on display, they created an immediate sensation. The Hall of Dinosaurs quickly became the most popular place in any museum, particularly for kids. It still is.

Do you remember the first time you went to the museum to see the dinosaur skeletons? I remember my first visit vividly, and still visit the Hall of Dinosaurs in the museum every

7

chance I get. It's still astonishing and wonderful.

By the early years of the twentieth century, dinosaurs were clearly big attractions. Dinosaur pictures, and models, and bones are fine, but they can't move. Making the prehistoric monsters move was the next step in the dinosaur's rise to stardom.

2

HOLLYWOOD DAYS

Imagine a dinosaur winning an Academy Award. There it would stand in the spotlight, clutching a tiny Oscar in its front claws. Choked with emotion the beast would deliver it's acceptance speech.

"And I would like to thank all the little people who helped me in my career. And most of all I would like to pay tribute to the memory of Willis O'Brien."

More than any other individual O'Brien (or O'Bie as most of his friends called him) was the man responsible for making dinosaurs into movie stars. O'Bie, who was born in California in 1886, had held a whole variety of jobs when he was young. The one he liked best was serving as a guide for scientists. The scientists were searching the Crater Lake region of California for fossils. Their work captured the young guide's imagination.

O'Bie also had a talent for making clay models. One day he and a friend molded some clay boxers. One man would model a boxer throwing a punch. The other would mold his boxer to defend against the punch. Since the clay was soft, they could move the arms and body of the models. From this an idea was born. Make a clay model and take a picture of it. Move it a little bit, and take another picture. Move it a bit more and shoot yet another picture. And so on. Then look at the pictures in rapid sequence. It would look as if the model was moving naturally. It was the same principle already being used in drawing animated cartoons.

O'Bie thought he might use the process to make films. In order to convince some producer that the process was worth putting money into, O'Bie needed a sample film to show them. But what subject would he use? He thought back to his fascination with prehistoric life. So he sculpted a model caveman and a model dinosaur. He got a friend who was a newsreel cameraman to film the models, one picture or one frame at a time. The process came to be known as "stop motion photography" or "stop motion animation."

The finished film ran less than a minute and a half. The movements looked jerky. The clay models began to melt under the lights. In short it was crude. But this was 1916—all film making was crude.

O'Bie found a San Francisco filmmaker who thought the stop motion idea had promise. He gave O'Bie $5,000 to make a short film using models. The result was the *Dinosaur and the Missing Link*. O'Brien improved his process. Instead of simple clay models he used rubber ones with jointed metal skeletons. The sets were more elaborate. Every leaf and pebble was glued carefully in place, so that they did not move when the models were moved. Filming took two months. The film itself ran only five minutes.

It took the San Francisco filmmaker about a year before he could find someone interested in distributing the film. Then he showed the *Dinosaur and the Missing Link* to the inventor Thomas Edison. Edison was one of the greatest inventors of his day. He invented the electric light bulb, the phonograph, and the motion picture camera. He also owned a company that made and distributed films. Edison loved *The Dinosaur and the Missing Link*. He bought it, and the film was finally shown to the public in May 1917. It was a big hit.

Edison hired O'Bie to make some more short films. Most of them were about "prehistoric" subjects. In one a couple of cavemen invent the wheel. But when they can't get a dinosaur to pull their cart, they give the whole thing up as a bad idea.

These early short films were strictly comedies. They didn't pay much attention to scientific accuracy. Then Edison had O'Bie make some educational films. He began working with scientists from the American Museum of Natural History to make sure his models were accurate.

While the films were a success the Edison company itself got into trouble and O'Bie was soon out of a job. A producer named Herbert Dawley then commissioned O'Bie to do another dinosaur film. It was called *The Ghost of Slumber Mountain*. The film mixed the animated figures with live actors. The small dinosaur models were made to look huge through the use of trick photography. The film was about a man who finds a hidden valley where dinosaurs live. In the end the whole adventure turns out to be a dream.

O'Bie's original film ran forty-five minutes. Dawley cut it to sixteen minutes, because he didn't think it would be a big hit. It was, and Dawley made over $100,000. He had paid O'Bie only $3,000. Worse still, Dawley tried to take all the credit for the animation. O'Bie was furious and refused to have anything more to do with Dawley.

Dinosaur models used in the 1923 version of *The Lost World*.

Then O'Bie got the first of two big breaks in his life. He teamed up with a producer named Watterson R. Rothacker. They decided that together they were going to make a film of *The Lost World*.

The Lost World is a book written by Sir Arthur Conan Doyle. Doyle is most famous for his character Sherlock Holmes. But Doyle wrote a lot of other books and stories. He created another popular character as well, the eccentric and terrible-tempered Professor Challenger. In *The Lost World,* Challenger leads an expedition to a remote part of South America, a place where dinosaurs still roam. It's the best of the Challenger novels, and still well worth reading today.

The Lost World was a perfect subject for O'Bie's special effects. Rothacker raised over $1 million to make the film. Today a "cheap" film costs $4 or $5 million, but this was 1923,

Triceratops model from *The Lost World*.

when films were being made for $4 or $5 *thousand!* The Lost World was one of the most elaborate and expensive films made up to that time.

For O'Bie and his small staff, making the film was an incredible job. There were over fifty dinosaur models. Each was sixteen to twenty inches long. Every model was built on a movable metallic skeleton that was padded out with sponge rubber and covered with a thick rubber skin. The models even contained rubber airbags which could be inflated and deflated to make it look as if the dinosaur was actually breathing.

The models looked more realistic than most of the actors in films of the time. For example, in a typical action film when the villain was shot or stabbed, he didn't bleed. He just died. O'Bie's dinosaurs would bleed when injured. He used chocolate syrup to simulate blood. In black-and-white, the brown syrup looked like blood. O'Bie also used shellac for dinosaurs that drooled.

The sets in which the model dinosaurs moved were usually about six feet long, by four feet wide. But the spectacular dinosaur stampede in the film required a 150-foot-long set.

O'Bie had help building the models and sets. But during the filming itself, he usually worked alone. In an average ten-hour day he could complete about 480 separate frames or pictures. That was just about thirty seconds of running time on the screen.

The Lost World wasn't all dinosaur models. It was a mixture of models and live actors. The well-known actor Wallace Beery played Professor Challenger. There were a tremendous number of special effects, and trick photography was used to make the model dinosaurs and live actors seem on the same scale. It was all very spectacular. There was a volcanic eruption and a dinosaur stampede. In one of the final scenes, a brontosaurus, brought back to London, breaks loose and levels all sorts of landmarks. This was the first of many "prehistoric monster loose in the city" scenes that were to become a familiar part of films.

If you could see the original version of *The Lost World* today it might look pretty silly. Films have come a long way since then in creating realistic looking special effects. But back in 1925 when the film was first released it was a sensation. Sir Arthur Conan Doyle was delighted with it. Before the film was shown to the public Doyle took a reel showing the dinosaurs in action to a meeting of the Society of American Magicians. He didn't tell the magicians or the press where the film had come from. Everyone was amazed. Some even thought the dino-

Scene from *The Lost World.*

saurs might be real. The next day *The New York Times* wrote that if the dinosaurs were fakes, "they were masterpieces."

When the film opened it was a huge success. It became one of the top moneymakers of its time.

So you can see that dinosaurs and Hollywood go back a long way together.

3

SKULL ISLAND

You might figure that with the huge success of *The Lost World*, Willis O'Brien and his dinosaurs had it made. But you would have figured wrong. In Hollywood, success is fickle. You can be a star one moment, and the next moment you can't even find a decent job.

After *The Lost World*, O'Bie started working on a film about the lost continent of Atlantis. There weren't going to be any dinosaurs in this one, but there were going to be some sea serpents that looked an awful lot like dinosaurs. And there were going to be some woolly mammoths. But after months of work, the project fell through.

O'Bie wanted to make a movie out of the Mary Shelley novel *Frankenstein*. He planned to have a human actor play the monster. But he would use his stop motion process for long shots. By using stop motion, O'Bie could have a model of the monster do things like pull up trees by the roots—the sort of thing no human actor could ever do. But O'Bie couldn't interest anybody in the project. Still, it was a good idea. Just three years later another studio made the *Frankenstein* movie with Boris Karloff, and it became a classic.

In 1930 O'Bie joined the RKO studio. RKO wanted him to do another explorer-meets-dinosaur film, like *The Lost World*. This one was going to be called *Creation*. It was to be the story of a submarine that gets shipwrecked on a volcanic island filled with dinosaurs.

For a year O'Bie made drawings, built models, and shot test scenes. Yet in the end the studio just dropped the project. There wasn't anything wrong with O'Bie's dinosaurs. Everyone agreed they were wonderful. But the picture was going to cost millions of dollars to make. The stop motion animation process was always time consuming and expensive. Now, however, movies were being made with sound. With sound films you had to shoot more frames per second. That made stop motion animation even more time consuming and expensive. RKO wasn't willing to risk millions of dollars. It looked as if a whole year of work had gone down the tubes. It looked like the end of the line for Willis O'Brien and his dinosaurs.

It wasn't the end of his career. In fact, the

biggest break that O'Bie ever got was just about to happen.

In 1929 the stock market crashed, and the Great Depression began. A lot of companies went out of business. Many more were in serious trouble. RKO was one of the companies in trouble. That's one of the reasons they didn't want to risk a lot of money on a project like *Creation*.

But the owners of RKO knew they had to do something, or they were going to go out of business. So they hired Merian C. Cooper, one of the boldest men in the history of films. Cooper had been a war hero, an aviator, and a first-rate newsreel cameraman. He had helped to produce a number of successful films. Then he went into the airline business and made a lot of money. But he got bored. He wanted to start making films again. So when he was asked to try to help the ailing RKO studio, he jumped at the chance.

Cooper had an idea about doing a movie about a giant gorilla. The Empire State Building had just been built. He envisioned a scene in which the gorilla would battle biplanes from the top of the world's tallest building.

Another news item attracted Cooper's interest. Giant lizards had been discovered on the tiny island of Komodo in the Pacific. The lizards were called Komodo dragons. Cooper thought that the giant gorilla might come from some lost island filled with giant lizards.

His first idea was to use a real gorilla made to look gigantic through the use of trick photography, and real lizards. But the more he thought about it, the more impractical the idea seemed. Gorillas probably wouldn't be very cooperative actors. The lizards would be even less cooperative.

When Cooper got to RKO he saw some of the test films for the ill-fated *Creation*. Suddenly he realized he didn't need real gorillas or real lizards. O'Bie could produce very realistic looking creatures through the use of his models.

The first title for the film was *The Giant Terror Gorilla*. It was finally renamed *King Kong*. *King Kong* was an enormous success. It saved RKO, and went on to become a classic. You've probably seen it.

King Kong is not, strictly speaking, a dinosaur film. There are, however, plenty of dinosaurs living in King Kong's realm on Skull Island. The *King Kong* story is well known. Movie producer Carl Denham, played by Robert Armstrong, sets out with his crew to make the ultimate animal picture. He has heard of a giant ape living on remote Skull Island. Ann Darrow (Fay Wray), who is supposed to play a leading role in the proposed film, accompanies the crew. When they reach the island,

Publicity shot shows producer Merian C. Cooper "imagining" a scene from *King Kong*.

Scene from *King Kong*.

they are captured by the natives, who offer Ann up as "Bride of Kong"—to be, in reality, a sacrifice. But the big ape falls for the little blonde. He carries her off to his lair with the movie crew in hot pursuit. It's while they are chasing Kong that they meet up with all the dinosaurs.

The first is a surprisingly aggressive stegosaurus that has to be driven off with gas bombs. Next is an apatosaurus. Scientists believe the apatosaurus was a peaceful plant eater. On

Skull Island it's a killer. It rises out of a steaming pool and turns over the raft on which Denham and his men are crossing the swamp. When it traps one member of the crew in a tree, the beast snatches him up for a meal.

A tyrannosaurus menaces Ann, and Kong rushes to the rescue. The king of the apes battles the king of the dinosaurs. Kong finally prevails by pulling apart the tyrannosaurus's huge jaws.

"Little Kong" prepares to battle a dinosaurlike creature in *Son of Kong*.

Scene from *The Giant Behemoth*.

Kong has to battle a couple of other monsters from the Age of the Dinosaurs. First is a sea-going reptile, the elasmosaurus. The elasmosaurus had a very long neck, but in *King Kong* it looks more like a snake with flippers. It wraps itself around Kong. He rips it off and beats it to death. A pterosaur swoops out of the sky to grab Ann. An enraged Kong tears it to shreds.

The enormously successful *King Kong* was quickly followed by a less ambitious sequel *Son of Kong*. It seems that when Kong rampaged through New York, a lot of people brought the bills for the things he broke to Carl Denham. In *Son of Kong,* a dead broke Denham returns to Skull Island looking for a treasure to pay off his debts. He encounters a smaller, friendlier albino version of Kong, and several prehistoric monsters. A number of them were left over from the original *King Kong*. The film is pretty funny, and was meant to be. This one was only a modest box office success.

Despite the enormous success of *King Kong,* and all the recognition it brought, the career of Willis O'Brien really slid downward after that high point. His dinosaurs appeared in other films, usually minor ones.

There was, for example, *The Beast from Hollow Mountain* (1955). This is essentially a Western with a dinosaur in it. The sheriff goes out to investigate the murder of a rancher. The killer turns out to be a carnivorous allosaurus that lives in a hidden cavern. The sheriff lassos the beast and brings it to town. But it escapes and ravages the countryside. Finally, the dinosaur is skewered by the sheriff with a gigantic stake.

O'Bie's final dinosaur film was *The Giant Behemoth* (1958). In this film, a brontosaurus-like creature smashes through London, and is finally done in by a radioactive torpedo.

O'Bie continued to work in films until his death in 1962. He never again attained the heights of *The Lost World* and *King Kong*. But for dinosaur lovers—indeed for all film buffs—these movies are triumphs that will never be forgotten.

4

THE ATOMIC DINOSAURS

When he was a young teenager growing up in California, Ray Harryhausen went to see the original *King Kong*. It changed his life.

Young Ray saw *King Kong* at the famous Grauman's Chinese Theater. His aunt was a nurse who had taken care of the invalid mother of the theater owner, Sid Grauman. The aunt was given three tickets to an afternoon performance. Since Grauman's was the most famous movie theater in the world in the 1930s, and *King Kong* was a very popular movie, the tickets were a real prize.

The boy was fascinated by the giant ape and the dinosaurs. He didn't know how the illusion of life had been created, but he thought that he had never seen anything so wonderful in his whole life. "These marvelous dinosaurs that

you'd seen in storybooks, and this gigantic ape
. . . simply overwhelmed me."

Ray had always been interested in dinosaurs
and other prehistoric creatures. He had often
drawn pictures of them. But here they seemed
to come alive on the screen. From that moment
Ray Harryhausen knew that what he wanted to
do more than anything else was create the same
sort of illusions he had seen in *King Kong*. He
learned about stop motion animation and began
making his own models. To make a cave bear he
cut up one of his mother's old fur coats. She
didn't mind. He also began shooting his own
films.

Ray was also interested in science fiction and
fantasy. He joined a science fiction club that
met once a week in a Los Angeles cafeteria.
While Ray Harryhausen was dreaming about
making stop motion films, another young member of the club, Ray Bradbury, was dreaming
about writing science fiction. The two Rays
became friends and shared their dreams. Years
later their careers were to come together in an
epoch-making film.

In the meantime, Ray Harryhausen began
taking courses in film making. He also began
planning a film about the story of life on earth—
particularly dinosaurs. It was to be called *Evolution*. In 1939, the young man gathered all his
courage and called his idol, Willis O'Brien.

O'Bie agreed to look at some of the work that Harryhausen had done on *Evolution*. O'Bie was very kind, and made a lot of good suggestions. One was "You've got to get more character into your animals."

Harryhausen labored at *Evolution* for another year. But finally he had to give it up. It was too big a project for one man. He got a job doing stop motion animation for cartoons. Then World War II came. Harryhausen wound up in an army film unit making training films.

After the war was over, some of the same people who had made the original *King Kong* film decided it was time to make another big ape film. This was about a giant ape captured in Africa and brought back to the United States. The film was called *Mighty Joe Young*. As a baby, the gorilla had been the pet of a family named Young.

Willis O'Brien was hired to do the stop motion animation for the gorilla. He asked Ray Harryhausen to work as his assistant.

Mighty Joe Young doesn't have any dinosaurs in it. It's certainly not another *King Kong*. Although it's played mostly for laughs, it's not really a bad film. Even after all these years, it's quite entertaining. However, it cost a lot of money to make. When it was first released in 1947 it was not a big hit, so it lost a lot of money. After that many producers were wary of

The rhedosaur attacks New York in *The Beast from 20,000 Fathoms.*

using stop motion animation at all. They thought it was too expensive, and that the public wasn't interested in that kind of film anymore.

It was years before Harryhausen got another good film project. But when he did, it was a

very good one. It was a film based on a story by his boyhood friend Ray Bradbury.

The story was called "The Beast from Twenty Thousand Fathoms" when it first appeared in a magazine. (When it later appeared in a collection of Bradbury short stories it was retitled "The Fog Horn," but the film producers went back to the more sensational original title.) It was a very short story about a dinosaur that lives deep in the ocean. The creature thinks it hears a mating call. When it comes to the surface it discovers that the noise is not coming from a lovesick female dinosaur, but is only a fog horn on a lighthouse. Disappointed and enraged, the dinosaur destroys the lighthouse and sinks back into the sea.

That is a very short story indeed. There is not enough in it to make a full-length film, so Harryhausen and the screen writers added a lot of details. Finally, the lighthouse fog horn became only an incident in the story. The most important added detail was the atomic bomb. This was the early 1950s, and people were just beginning to worry about the dangers of testing atomic bombs.

The film starts in the Arctic where the U.S. government is conducting atomic tests. Heat from the blasts releases a dinosaur that has been frozen in the ice for millions of years. The creature dives into the ocean and begins heading south. Along the way it destroys a fishing boat, a lighthouse (from the original story) and an entire New England fishing village. It's heading for its ancient breeding grounds—what is now New York City. The creature finally comes ashore around Wall Street. The beast crunches through lower Manhattan, stomping cars and buildings flat, and even swallowing a policeman whole. The army is called in, and with heavy artillery the soldiers are able to wound the creature in the neck. This, however, reveals a new danger. Its blood seems to contain some ancient but deadly disease. All who come in contact with the monster's blood, die. The creature can't be blown up or burned, for that would spread the germs far and wide, creating an even greater danger than the rampaging dinosaur itself.

The scientists who have been tracking the creature figure out a plan to kill it in relative safety. They will fire a small radioactive missile into the neck wound. The monster will then die from radiation poisoning, without spreading it's deadly blood any further.

After being wounded, the dinosaur goes back to the water. Then word comes that the creature has turned up again at Coney Island amusement park. A team of sharpshooters, armed with the radioactive bullets and dressed in radiation suits, begins stalking the beast. When they locate it, the creature is in the process of trashing the roller coaster. In order to get a clear shot, the sharpshooters ride to the top of the roller coaster. The shot is successful, but the monster does not die immediately. It thrashes around a lot, destroying the entire roller coaster in one of the best dinosaur death scenes in the history of the movies.

The creature in the film is called a rhedosaur. There is no dinosaur with that name. The beast looks more like a gigantic, toothy lizard than a real dinosaur. The rhedosaur appears to live in the sea; at least it is very much at home underwater. Real dinosaurs may have waded around in ponds and lakes, but they were basically land animals.

None of that really matters. *The Beast from 20,000 Fathoms* wasn't a scientific picture. It wasn't supposed to be. It was a thriller. An action film. The beast behaved and looked like we think a dinosaur should behave and look.

The producers watched their costs carefully. The film was made for a mere $200,000—a remarkably low figure even in those days. It looks like it cost a lot more to make. *The Beast from 20,000 Fathoms* became the surprise hit of 1953 and it made pots and pots of money.

In Hollywood a successful film usually inspires a host of successors and imitators. *The Beast from 20,000 Fathoms* was certainly no exception. Ray Harryhausen's next major film was *It Came from Beneath the Sea*. This film has the same general themes—atomic fears and monsters on the loose. This time the monster is a gigantic octopus. Its food supply in the Pacific Ocean has been destroyed by atomic testing. So it rises from the depths in searth of a new food supply—in San Francisco. There followed a string of other atomic created, or atomic released giants like the gigantic ants of *Them!* (1954) or giant prehistoric praying mantises in *The Deadly Mantis* (1957).

But certainly the most successful film inspired by *The Beast from 20,000 Fathoms* was not made in Hollywood, but in Tokyo. The film is, of course, *Godzilla* (1954). Think about the similarities. Godzilla, like the rhedosaur, is a dinosaurlike monster roused after millions of years by atomic bomb tests. While the rhedosaur looks sort of like a lizard, Godzilla looks sort of like a tyrannosaurus. Like the rhedosaur, Godzilla rises out of the sea and goes stomping around a city—New York for the rhedosaur, Tokyo for Godzilla. The rhedosaur has deadly blood, Godzilla has atomic breath.

Godzilla was so popular that it inspired a whole series of films and a flock of imitators, in Japan and elsewhere. But that's a story for the next chapter.

5

GODZILLA AND FRIENDS

Godzilla is a dinosaur that never was, and never could have been. He is an improbable monster, and an even more improbable hero. But oh my, how popular he has become!

Godzilla was "born" at the Toho movie studios in Tokyo, Japan in 1954. He was conceived of as a four-hundred-foot-tall, two-legged, green amphibious dinosaur with "atomic breath." The monster had been asleep in the deep since the Age of the Dinosaurs. Then atomic testing in the Pacific awakened him and he was off on a rampage. The film was called *Godzilla, King of the Monsters*.

There is no stop motion animation used in this film. Godzilla is simply a man in a rubber monster suit. But it is a good monster suit. The film uses a lot of well-made miniature sets.

Godzilla attacks Tokyo.

When Godzilla is seen stomping around a miniature city, it looks surprisingly realistic.

In the film, Godzilla first appears off the coast of Odo Island. Ships disappear mysteriously, and there are rumors of a gigantic monster from the deep. The creature is called Godzilla.

The film's producers undoubtedly thought it might have an appeal in America. They hired the American actor Raymond Burr to play reporter Steve Martin, who is one of the first to see the monster rise from the deep. The scenes with Burr were inserted in the American version of the film.

Godzilla isn't satisfied with destroying little islands for long. Soon he's in Tokyo chomping up trains and stomping down buildings. He's invulnerable to practically everything. It looks as if all Tokyo, perhaps even the entire world, will be stamped out by this angry four-hundred-foot-tall creature. But there is help. A scientist named Dr. Sarazowa has invented a machine which turns living things into dust. Godzilla gets too close to it and he is completely disintegrated.

Now you might figure that after a creature has been disintegrated there is no way to revive it. And if this monster movie had not turned out to be a real monster hit, you would have been right. But the film was a huge success in Japan. In America it became the most popular Japanese movie ever. If the producer had known how successful Godzilla was to become, they would not have killed him off so completely in the first film.

But there is a saying in Hollywood, "You can't keep a good monster down." The saying also holds true for Japanese filmmakers. The second Godzilla film was released in America in 1955. The title was a bit confusing, it was called *Gigantis, the Fire Monster*. Somewhere in the film someone explains that Gigantis is really Godzilla's "scientific name." So Gigantis is really Godzilla. But the "fire monster" in the title is neither. It's really another huge dinosaurlike survivor from the past, called Angurus.

The actor who played Angurus had a harder time than the actor who played Godzilla. Angurus was supposed to be a four-legged creature, so the poor actor had to crawl around on his hands and knees. If Godzilla looked sort of like a tyrannosaurus, Angurus looked sort of like one of the heavily armored dinosaurs such as ankylosaurus. However, Angurus had a lot of extra spines and horns, which also made him look a bit like a cross between a rhinoceros and a porcupine. Angurus has fiery breath to match Godzilla's atomic breath.

The Godzilla in this film is not supposed to be the "real" Godzilla who was destroyed in the first film. But he is a close relative who looks and acts exactly like the original. For all practical purposes this second monster *is* the original Godzilla.

It seems that Godzilla and Angurus don't really like one another. They are first found battling it out on a remote island. They carry their battle to a large city which is nearly destroyed by the conflict. Finally Godzilla wins, only to be buried in an avalanche of ice and snow.

Is this finally the end for the "King of Monsters?" What do you think? Of course not, because this sequel was a big hit, too.

While the writers at Toho studios were dreaming up new adventures for their new star Godzilla they dreamed up a new prehistoric monster as well. This one looked sort of like the ancient flying reptile pterandon, except that it was as big as an ocean liner and could fly at supersonic speeds. As it flew, it left behind an impressive trail of smoke. While Godzilla was "awakened" by an atomic blast, Rodan, or more accurately two of the species were hatched when their eggs were exposed to a hydrogen bomb explosion. As usual, ordinary weapons don't bother the monsters. It takes the eruption of a volcano to kill them off—at least until the next sequel.

For the third of the Godzilla films the producers brought in another famous monster—King Kong. What was he doing in Japan? Don't ask. The film title was straightforward enough, *King Kong vs. Godzilla* (1963). This was the film in which Godzilla really began to change. Perhaps the producers had been sitting in the audience during showings of earlier Godzilla films and listening to people cheer the monster. As far as the public was concerned, Godzilla wasn't a city-destroying monster anymore—he was a hero. And he wasn't to be taken too seriously either. *King Kong vs. Godzilla* is playing mainly for laughs. The two monsters go after one another like a couple of oversized professional wrestlers.

It must be pointed out that the King Kong in this film is not the Willis O'Brien model used in the original *King Kong*. The part is played by a man in a monkey suit. But this King Kong proved to be very popular, and got his own series of Japanese films.

Next it was *Godzilla vs. the Thing* (1964). The "Thing" was a giant moth called Mothra. This monster was already familiar to fans of Japanese monster films. It had starred in its own film *Mothra* (1961). In 1965 Godzilla teamed up with Mothra and Rodan, to battle the menace of *Ghidrah, the Three-Headed Monster*. Godzilla and Rodan were still fighting Ghidrah in *Monster Zero* (1965).

By now Godzilla films were rolling off the Toho studios assembly line so fast it was hard to keep up with them. Godzilla fought the Sea Monster in 1966, and in 1967 had a son, a rather cute little creature called Minya. In *Son of Godzilla,* father and son battle the giant prehistoric spider Spiega.

The all-time, all-star Japanese monster film was released in the U.S. in 1969 under the title *Destroy All Monsters*. Its original Japanese title would be translated as *Attack of the Marching*

Godzilla and Ghidrah, the three-headed monster.

Monsters, and it's more appropriate. This one is pure comedy fantasy. It features all of the familiar Toho monsters—Godzilla, Minya, Rodan, Mothra, Angurus, Spiega—a dinosaurlike creature called Gorosaurus, and others. There were dozens of actors sweating it out under heavy rubber costumes while this epic was being made.

Destroy All Monsters is set in the future. All the good monsters have been sent to live peacefully with one another on Monster Island. But then there is an invasion from outer space led by Ghidrah—one monster who never seemed able to reform. The monsters suddenly become monstrous again and threaten the world. But in the end they soften, and save humanity by driving the perpetually evil Ghidrah off the Earth.

You might imagine that after that epic Godzilla might retire to Monster Island for good. But no. The public demanded more, and they got more. The later Godzilla films were made with lower budgets and less care. They lacked the special effects and the wild imagination of earlier films. They simply are not as good, although Toho studios still came up with some very interesting monsters. In *Godzilla vs. the Smog Monster* (1972), Godzilla fights a shapeless, slithering, slimy creature that was created from pollution. In a 1975 film that was released

Angurus and Gorosaurus, more monsters from Japanese films.

under several different titles, Godzilla meets his robot counterpart Mechagodzilla.

In addition to the many films, there were Godzilla comic books, toys, T-shirts and all of the other signs of superstardom. Godzilla even had his own show on U.S. television, an animated cartoon series called "The Godzilla Power Hour."

By the mid 1980s Toho studios decided to remake the original Godzilla, in color and with a bigger budget. Segments with Raymond Burr from the original cast were even inserted for American audiences. That film was released in the U.S. under the title *Godzilla 1985*. It's flashier than the original, and fun to watch. But somehow it lacks the energy of the original. It just goes to show once again that it's hard to remake a classic.

With Godzilla in the lead, Toho studios dominated the booming Japanese monster movie market for decades. But other studios tried to cash in on the public appetite for movie monsters. Daiel Motion Pictures, another Tokyo-based company, created its own prehistoric monster, Gamera (or Gammera). Gamera doesn't really look like a dinosaur. He looks more like a gigantic, fire-breathing turtle with large tusks. Gamera walks on all fours, can stand up and walk on his hind legs, or will shoot off into the sky on jets of flame when really in a hurry. In the bizarre world of Japanese monsters, Gamera may be the strangest.

Gamera sounds like a monster from space. But according to the first film in the series, *Gammera the Invincible* (1966), the monster is just another one of those creatures from prehistoric times that got frozen into a block of ice and was thawed out by a nuclear blast. Soon Gamera is off destroying the countryside. Bullets, even rockets bounce off the creature's shell, and he eats fire.

As in other Japanese monster films, the lead was played by a man in a rubber monster suit. This actor had a chance to show some range. He could walk or crawl.

At the end of the film, Gamera is stopped but not destroyed. He is lured into a spacecraft and sent to Mars. Daiel studios must have figured that if the monster proved popular enough for a series it would be easier to bring him back from Mars than it would be to explain how he survived after being reduced to ashes. Gamera was a hit, and within a few months the flying turtle was back in *War of the Monsters*.

A meteor strikes the rocket carrying Gamera to Mars. The rocket is deflected back to Earth, and the giant turtle is once again on the loose. He meets up with another prehistoric reptile, one that has the ability to freeze anything that comes within the range of its row of electrically charged spikes. For more conventional warfare this monster, called Barugon, has a big horn on its nose and a tongue like a club.

By the third Gamera film, this one-time destroyer of the Earth and enemy of mankind had undergone the same sort of change that overtook Godzilla. He had become a good guy, who wants to save the Earth, not destroy it. There was a whole string of Gamera films made in the 1960s and early 1970s.

Gamera was never as popular as Godzilla

either in Japan or the U.S. In America Gamera films usually went directly to television, where they were shown on Saturday mornings. Sure, the pictures are usually silly and cheaply made. But the fire-breathing turtle and his monstrous foes are so strange looking, and the scripts are so wild and crazy, that the films still can be a lot of fun to watch. You can't help but laugh every time Gamera takes off and spins through the sky spouting flames in all directions like a crazed flying saucer.

Other Japanese studios tried to cash in on Godzilla's popularity. A South Korean–Japanese collaboration produced *Yongary, Monster from the Deep*. Yongary looks a lot like Godzilla, except he has longer spines on his back and he destroys Korean rather than Japanese cities. He successfully fights off the Korean army, but is killed by nerve gas. If there are any sequels, they have not been shown in the U.S.

Of all the Godzilla imitators, the best was probably Gorgo. The film was made in Britain in 1959. It features yet another man in a rubber monster suit. The theme of the film is the familiar prehistoric monster on the loose idea. The director was Eugene Lourie, the same man who directed *The Beast from 20,000 Fathoms* and *The Giant Behemoth*.

There are no atomic explosions here, however. An enormous prehistoric reptile is captured deep in the ocean. The creature, called Gorgo, is brought to London as a circus attraction. Gorgo is a dinosaurlike monster. Its most unusual features are finlike appendages where its ears should be.

Gorgo is huge, but after they get him to London his captors learn, to their horror, that he is only a baby, and Mommy is heading toward England to rescue him. She knocks over a large part of London before she finally finds the baby monster. They bellow a greeting to one another, and together stomp off back to the sea, crushing famous landmarks as they go.

Gorgo was a well-produced film. The actors were good, the color was excellent, and when the monsters are crashing through miniature sets it all looks very realistic.

Another man-in-a-rubber-reptile-suit film series should be mentioned at this point, *The Creature from the Black Lagoon* (1954) and two sequels made in 1956, *The Revenge of the Creature* and *The Creature Walks*. The creature, or Gill Man, as it is often called, is supposed to be a survivor from ancient times that is living in an isolated South American lagoon until disturbed by scientists. The Gill Man doesn't really look like a dinosaur and isn't supposed to. He is normal human size, rather than gigantic. But many of the familiar elements of the monster from the past films can be seen in the series.

Perhaps because the Creature films are rather simple and don't have to rely heavily on trick photography and special effects, they are surprisingly realistic. The original Creature film was also made in 3-D, a popular film gimmick of the 1950s that is revived occasionally. The audience is given special glasses with which to view the film. With the glasses the screen no longer looks flat, and in some scenes it appears as if the monster is swimming right out at you. Without the glasses, everything is blurry and you get a bad headache.

For a while the Gill Man was extremely popular, inspiring a line of comic books and toys. Even today Gill Man masks are sold around Halloween.

But none of these monsters ever came close to matching the great Godzilla in popularity.

6

LIZARDS IN COSTUME

As mentioned, the name dinosaur means "terrible lizard." The name really is not accurate. Many dinosaurs were peaceful plant eaters, and not very terrible. And they were not lizards—they are not even closely related to lizards or other modern reptiles.

Dinosaurs don't really look like lizards. Most dinosaurs walked on two legs. While there are a couple of modern lizards that can rear up on their hind legs, and even run short distances on them, most lizards keep their four feet firmly on the ground at all times. Even the four-legged dinosaurs, like the brontosaurus, don't look like modern lizards. The four-legged dinosaurs had straight, sturdy legs set firmly underneath their bodies. Modern lizards are sprawlers. Their legs are set wide apart. They move low to the ground, and they can flop down on their bellies as soon as they get tired. Just look at pictures of dinosaurs and compare them with pictures of modern lizards. They do not look alike.

But somehow we think dinosaurs *should* look like lizards. And for a very long time Hollywood filmmakers have made use of our general but quite incorrect impression that dinosaurs and lizards do look alike.

The technique of using lizards or other modern reptiles to impersonate dinosaurs in films started early in the history of the movies. Way back in 1914, the director D. W. Griffith, one of the pioneers of movie making, made a film about prehistoric life called *Brute Force*. It was a highly fanciful story about warring tribes of cave men. Griffith thought it would be a good idea to throw in a couple of "prehistoric-looking" animals, just to add to the atmosphere.

Filmmakers seem to think that if a creature has frills or spikes or horns, it looks prehistoric. One of the "prehistoric" animals in *Brute Force* was a snake with a sort of a crown on top of its head. Another was an alligator with a horn and wings that looked more like the mythical dragon than a dinosaur.

There was a dinosaur of sorts in this early film. It was a model of a two-legged, meat-eating dinosaur. It wasn't a very movable model. All it could do was rock back and forth, and open and close its jaws. Even in 1914, this was a poor example of special effects. *Brute Force* is not regarded as one of the great classics of the silent film era.

The most ambitious use of lizards and other animals in costume to portray dinosaurs came in the 1940 film *One Million B.C.* The film gets its history and science all mixed up. As seen in the film, the world about a million years ago was populated by very modern-looking cave men and women, prehistoric mammals like the woolly mammoth, and dinosaurs. It is hardly necessary to repeat that the dinosaurs died off millions and millions of years before either woolly mammoths or cave men ever appeared on earth.

The plot of *One Million B.C.* centers around the love of Tumak (Victor Mature) of the Rock tribe for the lovely Loana (Carole Landis) of the Shell tribe. As is traditional in films, the course of true love does not run smoothly. Many of the problems this cave couple encounters are caused by a variety of truly bizarre-looking beasts.

Early in the film, Tumak kills what appears to be a small triceratops. This creature is portrayed—amazingly—by a pig in a dinosaur outfit. Then Tumak is chased by a woolly mammoth. That was a comparatively simple job for

Lizards enlarged by trick photography played the part of dinosaurs in the original *One Million B.C.*

the costume department, just put a fur coat and phony tusks on a modern elephant. There was a musk ox, played by a bull in costume. The glyptodont, a giant ancestor of the armadillo, was played by a modern armadillo with rubber horns.

The most spectacular scene in the film is a fight between two "dinosaurs." One is a tegu lizard, the other a dwarf alligator with a large rubber fin attached to its back. Trick photography is used to make these rather small animals appear enormous.

In the film's final scene, the people of the Shell tribe are menaced by a giant *neecha*, their word for "giant monster." The *neecha* is a rhinoceros iguana also made to appear enormous through the use of trick photography.

A small tyrannosaurus makes a brief appearance in the film. Since there is no modern animal that could be costumed to successfully impersonate a tyrannosaurus, the part had to be played by a stunt man wearing a dinosaur suit.

Today the frilled lizards and horned armadillos of *One Million B.C.* look rather silly. The human actors in the film are even less convincing than the animals. But the film was quite popular when it first came out. Even today dinosaur film buffs consider it the best of the lizards-as-dinosaur films. Many of the scenes

Publicity still showing enlarged iguana menacing a caveman, played by Victor Mature, and a cavewoman, played by Carole Landis, in *One Million B.C.*

shot for this film turned up again and again as stock shots in cheapie films with names like *Untamed Women* (1952) and *Teenage Caveman* (1958) as well as on a number of television shows. Even the tyrannosaurus costume was used again in a couple of low-budget films.

Two other big-budget films tried to use the lizards-as-dinosaurs gimmick. One was *Journey*

to the Center of the Earth (1959). The film was based on the classic Jules Verne science fiction novel. In the novel the explorers go into the center of the earth, which turns out to be hollow. There they find a huge sea, and witness a fight between a couple of prehistoric marine reptiles. In the film the fight is between a couple of "dinosaurs." They are, in reality, two iguanas sporting rubber fins. The fight is filmed in slow motion.

In 1960 producer Irwin Allen announced that he was going to remake the silent classic *The Lost World* in lavish color. He even hired Willis O'Brien, who had created dinosaurs for the original *Lost World,* to oversee the special effects. O'Bie, who had been having a tough time with his career, was delighted. But he soon learned that the producer had no intention of using stop motion animation, a process which had proved to be too expensive and time-consuming. O'Bie had been hired just so his name could be put in the credits. He had almost nothing to do with the actual production of the film. This film was to use lizards as dinosaurs. They were a lot cheaper than stop motion models.

While *One Million B.C.* is effective, if a bit silly and artificial, the remake of *The Lost World* is a real disaster. And that's a real shame, because the human characters, particularly the fine actor Claude Rains, who plays Professor Challenger, are quite good. However, the lizards, with their plastic frills, are just not up to the task.

Perhaps the film would not have been quite so bad if the script writers had not insisted on having Professor Challenger name some of the dinosaurs he encountered. Challenger points out a "brontosaurus." Practically everybody in the audience knew what a brontosaurus was supposed to look like. The gigantic brontosaurus, with its long neck and tiny head, is perhaps the best known of all dinosaurs. The thing Challenger was pointing to was a monitor lizard with an artificial frill on its short neck. It didn't look in the least bit like the brontosaurus. The two-legged tyrannosaurus was another lizard with a plastic fin on its back and a horn on its nose. The real tyrannosaurus didn't have horns or fins.

This was not merely foolish, it was actually insulting to the audience. When we go to a dinosaur film, we know it's a fantasy, not a science lesson. We're willing to make a lot of allowances. But when someone says there is a brontosaurus or a tyrannosaurus, we have a right to expect that there will be some attempt to make the creature look like it's supposed to. In the remake of *The Lost World* the producer didn't bother.

The producer also didn't even attempt to have the spectacular final scene of the original, in which the brontosaurus runs amok in London. He just has Professor Challenger grab what is supposed to be a baby dinosaur and announce that he is taking it to London. Perhaps the producer thought that he could use the London scene in a sequel. But there never was

61

a sequel. This version of *The Lost World* sank into well-deserved oblivion.

Indeed, the use of lizards or other animals as dinosaurs has pretty well disappeared from movie making today.

7

DINOSAUR CLASSICS

During the 1960s the British company, Hammer Films, remade some of the old horror and fantasy classics. Many of these remakes were surprisingly good. Horror film buffs regard one of the Hammer remakes, *Dracula,* with Christopher Lee, as being nearly as good as the original *Dracula* starring Bela Lugosi. Hammer Films had the advantage of being able to use color, while most of the originals were in black and white. Hammer could also use more modern special effects techniques.

There is one Hammer remake that is universally regarded as being much better than the original. It is the Hammer version of *One Million B.C.* Hammer called its version *One Million Years B.C.* (1966) to set it apart.

One of the reasons the remake was better

than the original is that the original simply wasn't very good. But the Hammer version is good, not only in comparison, but because it is a visually exciting film in its own right.

One Million Years B.C. marked the film debut of the very beautiful Raquel Welch, as Loana of the Shell tribe. Raquel in her "prehistoric" costume, which looks like a furry bikini, became a popular pinup picture in the mid 1960s.

While the producers used Raquel Welch to sell the film to the public, they also really cared about the overall quality. Hammer was not known for spending a lot of money on its films. Indeed, they were famous for making films as quickly and as cheaply as possible. But the budget for *One Million Years B.C.* was generous for them. Producer Michael Carreas tried to spend the money wisely.

Rather than creating a simplified-sounding "prehistoric" language for the cave people, the producer decided that the film would have no dialogue at all. There were a few simple words, and an occasional grunt, but the film was essentially played out in pantomime. This was a very bold and effective move. Usually "prehistoric" dialogue sounds more foolish than primitive.

The film was shot on the bleak volcanic Canary Island of Lanzarote. That gave it a timeless feel.

Harryhausen's model of a gigantic turtle, archelon, in *One Million Years B.C.* was a triumph of realism.

A young cavewoman is menaced by a hungry allosaurus in *One Million Years B.C.*

But the best decision that Carreas made was to forget about the lizards used in the original and hire master stop motion animator Ray Harryhausen to provide the dinosaurs. The dinosaurs Harryhausen constructed for this film were the best he had ever done.

Early in the film one becomes a little nervous because the first two "monsters" to appear on the screen are a spider and an iguana. But they are a real spider and iguana simply made to appear gigantic. When the film was finished, the producer felt it needed a bit more excitement near the beginning. There wasn't the time nor the money to create new stop motion animation figures, so these "real" monsters were thrown in. They cheapen, but do not ruin the film.

There is other evidence of a tight budget and a tight shooting schedule. A model brontosaurus had been built for a scene in which it was supposed to attack Tumak's tribe. But by the time that scene was to be shot, the film was already running over budget and behind schedule, so it was dropped. The brontosaurus appears only briefly, lumbering across the desert. We wish we could have seen more of this creature.

The first stop motion monster to appear on the screen is a gigantic turtle. There really was a gigantic turtle called archelon, though it was not nearly as big as the one in the film appears to be. This model was so realistic that some critics complained that Harryhausen used a real turtle.

In what may be the best scene in the film, Tumak saves a young girl from a hungry allosaurus. Loana and Tumak are chased by a roving triceratops, but the horned dinosaur gives up the chase when it meets a ravenous ceratosaur. Loana is kidnapped by a flying pteranodon, who is about to feed her to its young. It is then attacked by another gigantic flying reptile, the tailed rhamphorhynchus. In the fight that follows Loana escapes.

All of these effects are exceptionally well done. While watching the film you know they are models, but they are so realistic that they still have the power to make you gasp.

One Million Years B.C. was an extremely popular film. It made a great deal of money and, as you might expect, it inspired a new rash of dinosaur films, some of them quite good.

Back in 1942 Willis O'Brien had begun work on a movie about a monstrous allosaurus that lived in a hidden valley in Mexico. O'Bie even had the allosaurus model built. Like so many of his projects, this one fell through. After his success with *One Million Years B.C.*, Harryhausen ran across the old script, the model, and some of the original drawings. He decided to bring the story to the screen. It was ultimately released as *The Valley of Gwangi* (1969).

The film is set in Mexico in 1912. There is a Forbidden Valley, which, according to legend, contains all sorts of prehistoric animals ruled by a gigantic dinosaur called Gwangi. Some of the local people consider the valley sacred. However, the valley is invaded by some cowboys from the T. J. Breckenbridge Wild West Show. They think that a dinosaur or two would make a great attraction for their show. As the cowboys proceed ever deeper into the Forbidden Valley, they first meet a pteranodon that swoops out of the sky and briefly captures one of the men. Then they see a small ostrichlike dinosaur, ornithomimus. While chasing the smaller dinosaur, they suddenly and startlingly encounter the gigantic allosaurus, Gwangi.

After a chase in which the cowboys try to lasso the allosaurus, and some fairly improbable events, the cowboys do manage to tie the beast up securely. It is hauled out to the city where it is put on display in a cage.

The gypsy witch Tia Zorina insists that the sacred Forbidden Valley has been violated. Her dwarfish assistant unlocks the monster's cage. Once again, it is a case of prehistoric monster loose in the city, this time a Mexican city. Along the way Gwangi kills an elephant from the Wild West show.

Finally, the monster is trapped in a cathedral. In its rage it kicks over a brazier of live coals. The cathedral drapes catch fire, the monster is burned to death, and the body is buried in the collapse of the building. It is a spectacular final scene.

The similarities between this film and *King Kong* and *The Beast from Hollow Mountain*, which also places an allosaurus in a Western setting, are obvious. But the scenes of Gwangi and the other dinosaurs in action are among the very best stop motion dinosaur sequences ever filmed. *The Valley of Gwangi* is worth seeing just for their sake.

In *The Valley of Gwangi*, cowboys meet dinosaurs.

Hammer made an attempt to duplicate the success of *One Million Years B.C.* with *When Dinosaurs Ruled the Earth* (1970). The plot, which is about warring tribes of cave men, is very nearly identical to that of *One Million Years B.C.* Raquel Welch was replaced by the equally beautiful Victoria Verti. Harryhausen was working on other projects, so his place was taken by a talented young animator named Jim Danforth.

Purists might argue that there was only one authentic dinosaur in *When Dinosaurs Ruled the Earth*. It was a chasmosaurus, one of the horned dinosaurs. But there were a number of other realistic marine or flying reptiles from the Age of the Dinosaurs. There were also some giant land crabs, and some creatures that looked more or less like dinosaurs. Overall, the special effects were excellent, and they earned an Academy Award nomination.

A nearly legendary dinosaur sequence appears in a film that is rarely shown today. The film is a documentary called *Animal World* (1954). It is supposed to show the development of animals from microbes to dinosaurs. Most of the film is made up of nature photography, some of it very good. But nobody remembers anything but the dinosaur scenes.

Ray Harryhausen did the animation and Willis O'Brien designed most of the models.

A scene from *Animal World* shows a newly hatched dinosaur.

There were scenes of dinosaurs laying eggs, and of dinosaur eggs hatching, but most of all there were scenes of dinosaurs fighting. They roared, clawed, and bit big chunks out of one another.

When the picture was previewed, many of the critics thought that the dinosaur fights were so violent and bloody that they would scare viewers. A couple of the most violent scenes were cut out after the previews.

In truth the scenes probably are too violent. Dinosaurs didn't spend all their time fighting one another. But Harryhausen and O'Bie consulted with a lot of scientists before making the film. Despite the sensationalism and violence, this twenty-minute sequence from *Animal World* may be the most scientifically accurate depiction of dinosaurs ever to appear in a commercial film.

8

DINOSAURS FROM THE HOLLOW EARTH

People who make movies about dinosaurs, or who write adventure stories about dinosaurs, face a big problem. In order to make the film or story interesting, you need to have both human beings and dinosaurs. The problem is that dinosaurs and human beings never lived at the same time. There may have been some form of human being on earth two or even three million years ago. But dinosaurs have been dead and gone for sixty-five million years.

So the problem is how to get the people and the dinosaurs in the same place at the same time in order to make an exciting story.

The most common way of overcoming this problem is to imagine some sort of "lost world." Explorers find a remote island or hidden valley where the dinosaurs have continued to exist. That's the theme of films such as *The Lost World,* and even *King Kong.*

Another common theme is the "monster from the past"—a dinosaur or dinosaurlike creature is suddenly revived or awakened from a sixty- or seventy-million-year sleep. In these cases, it's usually atomic energy that brings the beast back to life.

Audiences seem willing to accept the idea that cave men and dinosaurs shared the same world. They didn't, but the device has worked successfully anyway in lots of films such as *One Million Years B.C.*

Another theme is time travel—sending people millions of years back into the past to the time when dinosaurs lived. That idea is used more frequently in books and stories than in movies. There is also space travel, finding a planet which is inhabited either by dinosaurs or creatures that look exactly like dinosaurs. We'll talk more about that in a later chapter.

And then there is the idea of finding dinosaurs underground—either in some deep and unexplored cavern or inside the hollow earth. Some very famous dinosaur stories and films have used this idea.

Just saying the earth is hollow sounds ridiculous. And, of course, it is. We now know that the earth is solid, and that the core of the earth is so hot that it is actually molten. But a century or so ago, the theory that the earth might be hollow didn't sound so utterly fantastic. A lot of intelligent and responsible people thought that it might be.

The hollow earth idea was first picked up by the French writer Jules Verne. Verne is regarded as the father of science fiction. His book *A Journey to the Center of the Earth* was first published in 1864. It tells of the journey of Professor Von Hardwigg, his nephew, and a guide to the center of the hollow earth. They get inside the earth by climbing down through an extinct volcano. Verne had talked to an explorer who had actually climbed a long way down into an extinct volcano.

Much of the earth's interior in the Verne story is covered by a vast Central Sea. In the sea Von Hardwigg and his companions meet a couple of prehistoric monsters. One is "the world-renowned Ichtyosaurus or Great Fish Lizard." The other is "the Pleisoaurus . . . or Sea Crocodile." They are, of course, locked in a "titanic struggle." In stories, prehistoric monsters are always ill tempered and always fighting.

In Verne's day dinosaurs were barely known at all. But some of the marine reptiles from that era, like the ichtyosaurus and plesiosaurus,

were known. Their fossils had been discovered before those of dinosaurs. So naturally Verne put them in his book, though his descriptions of the monsters are entirely fanciful.

When in 1959 *A Journey to the Center of the Earth* was made into a movie, dinosaurs replaced the battling marine giants. The dinosaurs in the film were played by a couple of iguanas.

The hollow earth theme was also used by Edgar Allan Poe, but it was used most effectively by Edgar Rice Burroughs. Burroughs, most famous as the creator of Tarzan the ape man, wrote more than Tarzan stories.

In 1914 he wrote a book called *At the Earth's Core*. The hero, David Innes, uses a fantastic

Scene from the film *Journey to the Center of the Earth*. Once again, lizards were used to impersonate dinosaurs.

drilling machine, sort of an underearth submarine, to penetrate to the center of the earth. There he finds an inner world called Pellucidar. This world is filled with strange life, much of which looks like dinosaurs or creatures from the Age of the Dinosaurs.

"I saw them meet, open-mouthed, hissing and snorting, in their titanic and interminable warring."

Burroughs had a wild imagination. In Pellucidar there are the Mahars. They resemble the winged reptiles called pterasaurs. But the

A couple of prehistoric creatures battle in *At the Earth's Core*.

Mahars are extremely intelligent—much more intelligent than the stone age humans who live in the Pellucidar.

The book was extremely popular, so in 1915 Burroughs came back with another inner world story called simply *Pellucidar*. Over the years

he wrote about half a dozen Pellucidar novels, and a number of short stories about the world inside the earth. One of the novels was called *Tarzan at the Earth's Core*. In this book the "Lord of the Jungle" has to go to the inner earth to rescue David Innes.

A British film company made *At the Earth's Core* into a film in 1976. The film was produced on a limited budget, so the special effects do not match Burrough's imaginative descriptions. The prehistoric creatures are really actors in rubber monster suits—and they look it. Many Burroughs fans were disappointed by the film. True enough, the book is much more exciting and imaginative than the film, although the film is not at all bad. If you liked the prehistoric monster costumes in *Godzilla* and other Japanese monster films, you will certainly enjoy *At the Earth's Core*.

Burroughs was fascinated with the idea of locating a prehistoric dinosaur-filled world somewhere, and he returned to the theme time and again. He wrote stories with names such as "The Cave Girl." But the best of his novels about dinosaurs are *The Land That Time Forgot,* and its two sequels, *The People That Time Forgot* and *Out of Time's Abyss.*

The Land That Time Forgot starts during World War I. An American named Bowen Tyler, Jr., has captured a German U-boat. While trying to escape with his prize, he finds a legendary island. The island is called Caprona and is a land filled with dinosaurs. When Tyler and his companions build a fortress to protect themselves, they christen it Fort Dinosaur.

Both *The Land That Time Forgot* and *The*

Scene from *The Land That Time Forgot.*

People That Time Forgot were made into films in the mid 1970s. As pure adventure yarns, they are pretty exciting. There are certainly plenty of dinosaurs in these films. But, unfortunately, the creatures, which are either rod puppets or mechanical constructs, are unrealistic and rather disappointing. The original novels are much, much better, and many people consider them the best books Burroughs ever wrote.

The prehistoric world under the Earth was also the theme used in a made-for-TV film called *The Last Dinosaur*. An oil drilling team discovers a primeval world beneath the polar ice cap. The oil company is owned by the world's richest man, Masten Thrust. Thrust, a big-game hunter, leads an expedition into this underground world. The expedition encounters a variety of creatures, including a tyrannosaurus, which is "the last dinosaur."

Though most of the cast of this film is American, the film was made in Japan, and the tyrannosaurus is a man in a monster suit who looks and sounds a lot like Godzilla.

9

CARTOONS AND COMICS

Who was the first star of an animated cartoon? Mickey Mouse? Bugs Bunny? Felix the Cat?

It's none of the above. The first character specially created for an animated cartoon was a lovable brontosaurus called Gertie.

The cartoon *Gertie the Dinosaur* was dreamed up in 1912 by Winston McCay. McCay was already a well-known cartoonist whose work appeared in newspapers all over the country.

The original version of "Gertie" was quite unusual. Back in 1912 there were few regular movie theaters. McCay used his cartoon as part of a stage performance. The artist would appear on the side of the stage. The cartoon would be projected on a large screen, and the real life artist would appear to be talking to his own cartoon dinosaur, and even tossing her food.

The original Gertie the Dinosaur.

Gertie proved to be enormously popular with audiences. In 1914 McCay prepared another version of the cartoon. This one could be shown on its own and did not have to be part of a stage show. The new *Gertie the Dinosaur* began with a live action sequence that was supposed to explain why McCay had created the character in the first place. According to this version the artist was inspired by a visit to the dinosaur hall of the American Museum of Natural History in New York City. McCay made a sequel called *Gertie on Tour* in 1917. Other cartoonists shamelessly appropriated the popular dinosaur for their animated cartoons, and there were several *Gertie the Dinosaur* books for children.

So Gertie was the first cartoon dinosaur—but by no means the last. Dinosaurs of one sort or another began to appear regularly in cartoons along with such popular characters as Felix the Cat, Betty Boop, Daffy Duck, Porky Pig, and Mighty Mouse.

But when it comes to dinosaur cartoons there is one that stands far, far above all the rest. It is *The Rite of Spring* sequence from the 1940 Walt Disney movie *Fantasia*. Disney got the idea of doing animated cartoon interpretations of various pieces of classical music after talking to a well-known symphony orchestra conductor. For the piece of music called *The*

Sorcerer's Apprentice, Mickey Mouse appears as a bumbling magician's assistant who unleashes a horde of water-toning brooms. In the spooky section called *A Night on Bald Mountain,* all manner of ghostly and demonic creatures are seen awakening for nighttime revels.

The Rite of Spring was written by the composer Igor Stravinsky. The composer thought of his music as suggesting some sort of primitive tribal ceremony. The Disney animators decided that the music could suggest a far grander scene. The sequence begins with the creation of the earth. It moves quickly to the appearance and evolution of life. It is the Age of the Dinosaurs that dominates this trip through time.

Disney created a stunning variety of dinosaurs for the screen. At first they are seen engaged in feeding and other peaceful activities. Then, with a flash of lightning and crack of thunder, the monstrous *Tyrannosaurus rex* appears. The other dinosaurs try to flee, but the stegosaurus is too slow to make its escape. In a terrifying battle it is killed by the tyrannosaurus.

The battle is the high point of the sequence. After that, time moves on swiftly. The world changes, becoming hotter and drier. The dinosaurs are seen desperately and unsuccessfully

The Rite of Spring, from the Walt Disney classic *Fantasia.*

searching for water. Finally, all that is left of them are bones; and these too are covered up by the blowing sand.

Though the tyrannosaurus is one of the most frightening creatures ever to appear in a film, this is no mere dinosaur as monster cartoon. The Disney animators made a reasonable attempt to be scientifically accurate. All of the dinosaurs shown are creatures that once existed. There are no imaginary dinosaurs.

The creators of *Fantasia,* on the other hand, did take some leeway with the facts. The stegosaurus was probably extinct before the tyrannosaurus ever appeared, so that gigantic battle could not have taken place. Our view of the end of the Age of the Dinosaurs has changed greatly since 1940. If the film were to be made today the section might end with a gigantic meteorite hitting the earth.

But none of this criticism really matters. *The Rite of Spring* is beautiful, moving, and frightening, all at once. It is not only the best representation of dinosaurs in an animated cartoon, many people think it is the best representation of dinosaurs in any film of any kind ever. It is quite simply a dinosaurian masterpiece.

Ray Harryhausen was working on his projected film *Evolution* when he first saw *Fantasia.* After he saw *The Rite of Spring* he gave up the project he had been working on for a year. He knew that the dinosaurs in *Fantasia* were better than anything he could produce with stop motion animation.

Fantasia itself was a box office failure when it was first released. Some critics complained that the classical music was too "highbrow" for the average moviegoer. Others complained that the cartoons were too "lowbrow" for the lover of classical music. There were those who thought that some of the scenes, such as *The Rite of Spring* were too frightening for small children. But since 1940 the film has been re-released regularly, and it seems to gain a new and larger audience every time it is shown. *Fantasia* is now right up there with *Snow White* and *Pinocchio* as one of the truly great Disney films.

In 1985 the Disney studios once again tried to use dinosaurs in a film. This time it wasn't a cartoon, but a live action film with the dinosaurs produced by stop motion animated models and other special effects. The film was called *Baby!*

The story was based on the persistent rumors that some sort of dinosaurlike creature is still alive today in the central African swamps. It's really a variation of the lost world theme. There are good young scientists who try to rescue the baby brontosaurus from the clutches of an older bad scientist who wants to exploit it.

A baby brontosaurus is the central character in the film *Baby*.

The dinosaur models in the film are quite effective, and the baby dinosaur has a genuinely cute personality. But overall the film is a major disappointment. All the situations and characters are obvious and predictable. It's a modern film, but it looks old and dated. There is a lot of action, but none of it is really exciting. While the film is certainly not awful, we had expected a lot more from the studio that gave the world *Fantasia*.

While on the subject of dinosaurs in animated cartoons, we should mention, at least briefly, some of the dinosaurs that have appeared in the newspaper comics and comic books. Dinosaurs have always been extremely popular subjects in the comics. In the 1930s and 1940s everyone knew the long-necked, spiky-backed Dinny, dinosaur friend and companion of the cave man Alley Oop. *Alley Oop* was the grand daddy of all the cave man comics that were to follow. This rather brutish-looking fellow, his girl friend Oola, Dinny, King Guz, and a host of other characters, human and dinosaur, lived in the stone age kingdom of Moo. Later, time travel was introduced to allow Alley Oop and his friends to operate in a wider variety of environments.

The current king of stone age comics is cartoonist Johnny Hart's *B.C.* In this comic strip the cave men live in a world with dinosaurs, anteaters, ants, snakes and turtles—and they all talk.

Both *Alley Oop* and *B.C.* have been featured in animated television specials, and the *B.C.* characters appear regularly in commercials.

There have also been a large number of brawny cave men, or Tarzan-type heroes, who either live in a fantasy prehistoric world filled with dinosaurs, or in a fantasy jungle world that is also filled with dinosaurs. The heroes of these comics have names like Kona, Monarch of Monster Isle; Naza, Stone Age Warrior; and Ka-Zar, Lord of the Hidden Jungle. Many of these comic books are quite ordinary, one looking and sounding very much like another. But a few of these comics were created by truly fine artists like Frank Frazetta and Wally Wood. Original versions of these comics have become extremely expensive collectors items today.

From time to time all of the standard comic superheroes—Superman, Spider Man, Plastic Man, Captain Marvel—have been forced to confront, and generally overcome, dinosaurs in one setting or the other.

Even that eternal teenager Archie and his friends have appeared in comic books set in a dinosaur-filled stone age.

10

DINOSAURS ON TV

Just as they were pioneers in the movies, dinosaurs were television pioneers as well.

It was very tough to put a dinosaur on TV in the early days. In early films the directors could use stop motion animation and a variety of camera tricks. But television in the beginning was done live, just like a stage show. If the special effects failed, there was no chance to reshoot and get it right the second or third time. And the early TV shows also had to be produced on tight budgets.

Science fiction shows were among the earliest to come to TV. In some of these first science fiction series, the adventurers would land on planets supposedly inhabited by dinosaurlike monsters. Often these monsters looked remarkably stiff. That's hardly surprising because they were simply plaster models on wheels that were pushed around by an unseen stage hand. For more elaborate special effects, the shows would use a model with jaws that could open and close, or a neck that moves back and forth. Very often the models were so cheaply made that the viewers could actually see the wire that operated the jaws or neck.

The directors made sure you didn't see the models for an extended period. A quick glimpse was usually enough. The heroes of these early shows spent a lot of time shooting at monsters that remained suspiciously just beyond camera range. The dialogue would run something like this:

"There it is Jack, shoot!"

"Zap."

"Got it."

The viewer never actually saw the thing that was being shot.

One series came up with a very clever gimmick. The heroes used ray guns which paralyzed the monsters. It was a simple way of explaining why the monsters didn't move.

More sophisticated shows used hand puppets—and miniature scenery—for the head and neck of a dinosaur. The puppets looked like puppets but they were better than a dinosaur statue on wheels.

No one was going to be fooled by these devices into thinking the dinosaurs were real. But, as in the early days of movies when the special effects were also quite crude, the audience didn't worry much about realism. They were just amazed that pictures appeared on the screen at all.

As television technology progressed, shows were able to insert stock scenes from old movies into live action shows. A dinosaur fight that was shown in the "Jungle Jim" series would have looked very familiar to anyone who had already seen the film *One Million B.C.*

Dinosaurs, usually represented by stock movie scenes, showed up regularly in such series as "Voyage to the Bottom of the Sea" and "Time Tunnel."

The head of a model dinosaur built for a forgettable film called *Tyrannosaurus* wound up in television. It was used as the dragonlike pet Spot in the 1960s comedy series "The Munsters."

But without any doubt, the most successful of all the TV shows in which dinosaurs were featured, is the long running cartoon series "The Flintstones." The series is a blend of the TV comedy of Jackie Gleason's popular series "The Honeymooners," and the stone age comedy of the old *Alley Oop* comedy strip. A lot of the "stone age" humor came from showing "prehistoric" creatures doing modern tasks.

The head from this dinosaur model used in the film *Tyrannosaurus* wound up as the dragonlike pet, Spot, in the TV series "The Munsters."

For example, Fred Flintstone works in a rock quarry. Instead of using modern power machinery to lift and crush the rocks, Fred's "machine" is a huge brontosaurus that looks and acts very much like a power shovel. The characters in "The Flintstones" don't eat hamburgers, they eat "brontoburgers."

However, dinosaurs are not merely beasts of burden or food for the Flintstones. The family has a pet, a small dinosaur of unknown species, called Dino. His name is a combination of the word dinosaur and Fido, a name commonly used for dogs. Dino acts a lot more like a dog than a dinosaur. He even barks. But he was probably the most famous and popular television dinosaur of his day. Indeed, he's probably still the most famous and popular television dinosaur, for "The Flintstones" series is rerun endlessly in syndication, and the characters, including Dino, still appear in TV ads.

As with most successful TV series, there were a large number of Flintstone products. Not only were there Flintstone comic books, for a while, Dino had his own comic book. There were also models and toys of Dino and the other Flintstone characters. Even Flintstone vitamins had one shaped like Dino.

The enormous success of "The Flintstones" encouraged the producers, Hanna-Barbera, to create other series with prehistoric themes. The most interesting was an animated series called "Valley of the Dinosaurs." It was about a family, The Butlers, who get lost while exploring the Amazon River in South America. They find an unknown valley inhabited by cave men and, of course, dinosaurs. "The Flintstones" was strictly stone-age comedy. There was no attempt to make the dinosaurs look realistic. While basically a cartoon adventure show, "Valley of the Dinosaurs" did try to present more scientifically accurate dinosaurs. The show, however, never attained anywhere near the popularity of "The Flintstones."

Undoubtedly, the most ambitious of all the dinosaur TV series, was "Land of the Lost." It first appeared in 1974, the same year as "Valley of the Dinosaurs." That was a banner year for dinosaurs on television.

Like "Valley of the Dinosaurs," this series also uses the family-in-a-lost-world-full-of-dinosaurs theme. The Marshalls are taking an ordinary rafting trip when they are suddenly caught up in a "dimensional vortex." Just exactly what a "dimensional vortex" is, is never explained, and probably never could be. Whatever it is, they wind up in a strange prehistoric world filled with cave men and, of course, dinosaurs. Unlike "Valley of the Dinosaurs," however, "Land of the Lost" was not a cartoon. It was a live action series. The producers were Sid and Marty Krofft, who had started out as puppeteers.

The dinosaurs in the series were stop motion animation models, some of which had originally been built for the movies. On the small television screen they were extremely effective.

"Land of the Lost" had regular dinosaur characters, and there was an attempt to give individual dinosaurs distinct personalities. There was the cute but clumsy baby brontosaurus called Dopy, a triceratops called Spike, and a tyrannosaurus named Grumpy, who was a good deal more threatening than his name would indicate.

For its first season, "Land of the Lost" was a high-quality series. Sure, many of the situations were familiar, and the dinosaurs a bit too cute. But the writers tried to keep the stories fresh and the special effects reflected thought and care. The result was that the show got very high ratings.

As we have mentioned before, however, good stop motion animation is expensive and time-consuming. By the second and third seasons there was less of the dinosaurs, and the overall quality of the special effects declined sharply. Whatever plot inspiration had been present during the first season began to dry up as time went on. The plots became more bizarre, but not really more interesting. Ultimately the series never fulfilled its early promise. But "Land of the Lost" still remains the most ambitious attempt to use dinosaurs in a television series.

Dinosaurs have also been featured in a variety of educational and scientific specials. Usually these shows use films of dinosaur skeletons in museums. However, a special called "Dinosaur" narrated by Christopher Reeve (the actor who played Superman in the movies), featured some really fine stop motion animation dinosaurs. This hour-long program was also notable because it attempted to bring viewers up-to-date on all the recent discoveries about dinosaurs. It was first shown in 1985, and has been rerun since. If you have not seen it, try to catch it next time around.

You wouldn't think that dinosaurs played much of a part in radio. After all, dinosaurs didn't talk. But even in this part of the world of entertainment, dinosaurs have had an impact.

In the days before television there was a great deal of original radio drama. Many of the adventure series featured heroes like Superman or Captain Midnight. Sometimes these heroes would get themselves involved with dinosaurlike creatures in a lost land or on some other planet. The dinosaurs made their presence known by hissing and roaring and crashing noisily through the underbrush.

Besides the regular series dramas there were

also anthology series. Each week the series would present a different complete radio drama. Sometimes the series would have a theme. There were mystery series, science fiction series, and so forth. Some really excellent dinosaur stories were dramatized on some of these series. It was all done with dialogue and sound effects, and the imagination of the listener. Sometimes what you can imagine is far more terrible and wonderful than what you actually see.

The day of radio dramas is now long gone. But those of us who listened to some of the dramas when we were kids will never forget them.

11

DINOSAURS FROM SPACE

Dinosaurs have so captured our imagination that when we think of some sort of alien monster, as often as not we picture it looking like a dinosaur. Certainly Hollywood has felt that way, for dinosaurs or dinosaurlike creatures have played a large part in science fiction films.

Take the 1957 film *Twenty Million Miles to Earth*. It begins with an expedition returning from the planet Venus. However, something goes wrong and the spaceship crashes into the Mediterranean. There is only one survivor. No, there are two survivors. One is the captain of the spaceship. The other is a tiny Venusian, packed in a metal cylinder.

The cylinder is washed ashore, where it is found by some Italian boys playing by the sea. When it is opened, a tiny Venusian crawls out.

The dinosaurlike Ymir from Venus battles an elephant in the film *Twenty Million Miles to Earth.*

The thing is placed in a cage, but by the next morning it has grown to the size of a human being, and breaks out of its cage.

The creature is called the Ymir. It looks like a two-legged reptile. More than anything else it looks like a dinosaur.

The Ymir was a Ray Harryhausen creation. Many science fiction film buffs consider the Ymir the greatest creation of this master of stop motion animation. The Ymir is no mindless destruction machine. Though the creature ultimately causes a great deal of destruction, it's not trying to be evil. It's simply trying to survive in an alien and hostile world. We don't hate the creature, we feel sympathy for it—much of the time we're actually rooting for it. That's the quality that sets this film above many other alien-monster-on-the-loose films. It's the same sort of sympathy that we feel toward the Frankenstein monster when we watch that film classic. But the Frankenstein monster was played by an actor, and a good one, Boris Karloff. The Ymir was an eighteen-inch-high model! Yet Harryhausen was so skillful that he really makes the thing come alive.

Exposed to the oxygen-rich atmosphere of earth, the Venusian creature grows explosively until it is twenty feet tall. The Ymir is pursued by farmers, townfolk, scientists, and soldiers. It is finally captured and taken to Rome. But the

Ymir breaks free from the laboratory in which it is being held. After killing a circus elephant in a monumental battle, the creature runs through the streets of Rome. (In the later film *The Valley of Gwangi* Harryhausen has a fight between a dinosaur and an elephant.) It is finally trapped and killed in the Colosseum in a spectacular and touching scene. That scene will remind you of King Kong atop the Empire State Building.

During the 1960s, the heyday of the popularity of the Godzilla films, many of the dinosaurlike monsters were supposed to have come from outer space. Later, in the popular space-horror film *Alien* (1979), the monster is never seen clearly. But from glimpses, one gets the feeling that it is distinctly dinosaurlike. Some of the monsters of the Star Wars films are also reminiscent of dinosaurs.

The idea that space travelers would discover a "prehistoric planet" inhabited by dinosaurs has been a common theme in science fiction stories. Looking through old science fiction magazines, it's revealing to see how often pictures of dinosaurs and spacemen appeared on the cover. Sometimes the pictures were on the cover even when there was no story about dinosaurs inside. Dinosaurs have always been good for sales.

Planet of the Dinosaurs (1977) is about a party of space travelers stranded in a world that looks very much like what we think earth looked during the Age of the Dinosaurs. The "prehistoric" planet is overrun with dinosaurs who make life difficult for the stranded travelers. The plot is a familiar one—it's *The Lost World,* set in outer space. But the animated dinosaurs are surprisingly good for a low budget film.

Is it possible that someday in the distant future space travelers on earth will land on a "prehistoric" planet somewhere, and human beings will once again encounter living dinosaurs? Unfortunately, that is highly unlikely. We may find very large, very strange creatures on other planets, but we can be almost certain that the dinosaurs were unique to our planet.

They first appeared on earth about 250 million years ago. For over 150 million years they were the most powerful creatures on the planet. Then, sixty-five million years ago, they all died out mysteriously and completely. But their images have been recreated for us time and again on the movie screen.

In the final chapter you will find a listing of some of the best dinosaur films ever made.

DINOSAUR FILMS

Dinosaur films shows up regularly on television. They are usually shown on Saturday afternoon, or on late-night series that feature monster and science fiction films. The classics, such as the original *King Kong,* or more recent films like *Baby,* are also widely available on videocasette.

Animal World (1954). Director, Irwin Allen. This is basically a nature film with a twenty-minute segment on dinosaurs. The stop motion animation was done by the two masters of the craft, Willis O'Brien and Ray Harryhausen.

At the Earth's Core (1976, British). Director, Kevin Conner. Stars: Doug McClure, Peter Cushing. Discovery of a "prehistoric world" inside the hollow earth. This is an adaptation of an Edgar Rice Burroughs novel. The film has a host of bizarre-looking creatures played by actors in monster suits.

Baby (1985). Director, B.W.L. Norton. Stars: William Katt, Sean Young, Patrick McGoohan, Julian Fellows. Discovery of dinosaurs living in a remote African swamp. The special effects are fine, but this film from the Walt Disney studios is disappointing.

The Beast of Hollow Mountain (1956). Director, Edward Nassour. Stars: Ismael Rodriguez, Guy Madison. A Western, a mystery, and a dinosaur film all in one. And a very nice combination, too.

The Beast from 20,000 Fathoms (1953). Director, Eugene Lourie. Stars: Paul Christian, Paula Raymond, Lee Van Cleef. The first of the "atomic monster" films. Ray Harryhausen's rhedosaurus is a classic.

Caveman (1981). Director, Carl Gottlieb. Stars: Ringo Starr, Jack Gilford, Shelly Long. Stone age comedy about a tribe of misfits, headed by ex-Beatle Ringo Starr. The jokes are not that funny, but the comic dinosaurs created by David Allen make the film very worthwhile.

Creature from the Black Lagoon (1954). Director, Jack Arnold. Stars: Richard Carlson, Julia Adams, Richard Denning. This isn't really a dinosaur film, but the Gill Man was "prehistoric" and reptilian. A good monster film followed by two lesser sequels. Originally filmed in 3-D.

Destroy All Monsters (1968, Japanese). Director, Inoshiro Honda. Stars: Akira Kubo, Jan Tazaka, Kyoko Ai. Toho studios all-star monster film, with Godzilla, Rodan, and the rest of the old gang.

Dinosaurus (1960). Director, Irvin S. Yeaworth, Jr. Stars: Ward Ramsey, Paul Lukather, Kristin Hanson. Cavemen and dinosaurs on a tropical island.

Fantasia (1940). The Walt Disney classic. *The Rite of Spring* segment is probably the best and most dramatic film representation of dinosaurs ever. A real masterpiece.

Gamera the Invincible (1966, Japanese). Director, Noriaki Yuasi. Stars: Brian Donlevy, Albert Dekker. The first of the series of films featuring the jet-propelled, prehistoric turtle.

The Giant Behemoth (1959, British). Director, Eugene Lourie. Stars: Gene Evans, Andre Morell. A standard prehistoric-monster-on-the-loose film with good special effects.

Godzilla, King of Monsters (1954, Japanese). Directors, Terry Morse, Inoshiro Honda. Stars: Raymond Burr, Takashi Shimura. The first of this fantastically popular series. Godzilla is destroyed at the end, but don't worry. He comes back again, and again and again.

Godzilla 1985 (1985, Japanese). Directors: Kohji Hashimoto, R.J. Kitzan. Stars: Raymond Burr, Keiju Kobayashi. A not entirely successful attempt to recreate the excitement of the original Godzilla film with up-to-date movie technology.

Gorgo (1961, British). Director, Eugene Lourie. Stars: Bill Travers, William Sylvester, Vincent Winter. One of the best monster-on-the-loose films;

this time it's in London. Effective use of actor in a rubber monster suit.

Journey to the Center of the Earth (1959). Director, Henry Levin. Stars: James Mason, Pat Boone, Arlene Dahl. Jules Verne's fantasy-adventure. Uses a couple of lizards for the great monster fight.

King Kong (1933). Directors, Merian C. Cooper, Ernest B. Schoedsack. Stars: Fay Wray, Bruce Cabot, Robert Armstrong. This is it! The original classic. Don't be fooled by later remakes. Both Kong and the dinosaurs were created by Willis O'Brien. The videocassette version contains some scenes that were cut from the versions shown on television.

The Land That Time Forgot (1975, British). Director, Kevin Connor. Stars: Doug McClure, John McEnry. A submarine discovers a prehistoric island during World War I. The film is based on an Edgar Rice Burroughs novel. The adventure is fine but the special effects are cheap and it shows.

The Lost World (1925). Director, Henry Holt. Stars: Bessie Love, Wallace Beery. Based on the novel by Sir Arthur Conan Doyle, this is the first great dinosaur film. It is also the first film to make extensive use of the talents of Willis O'Brien.

The Lost World (1960). Director, Irwin Allen. Stars: Claude Rains, Michael Rennie, Jill St. John. A remake of the silent film using real lizards instead of stop motion animation dinosaurs. Despite color and a good cast the film does not come anywhere near the original.

A brontosaurus attacks London in *The Lost World*.

One Million B.C. (1940). Director, Hal Roach. Stars: Victor Mature, Carole Landis, Lon Chaney, Jr. This is the king of the dinosaur impersonator movies. There are lizards, alligators, even a pig, dressed up as prehistoric creatures. Stock footage shot for the film appears in a dozen or more lesser films and in early TV shows.

One Million Years B.C. (1966, British). Director, Don Chaffey. Stars: Raquel Welch, John Richardson, Percy Herbert. Hammer studios superior remake of the 1940 cave man vs. dinosaur epic. Film contains some of the best Ray Harryhausen dinosaurs.

Planet of the Dinosaurs (1977, British). Director, James Aupperle. Stars: Harvey Shain, Pamela Buttaro, Chuck Pennington. Adventures on a prehistoric planet. Excellent stop motion animation by Douglas Beswick.

Reptilicus (1962). Director, Sidney Pink. Stars: Carl Ottosen, Ann Smymer. A dinosaurlike monster in space. Actually it was filmed in Denmark, and is good for a laugh.

Rodan! (1957, Japanese). Director, Inoshiro Honda. Stars: Kenji Swara, Yumi Shirakawa. Next to Godzilla himself, Rodan, the flying prehistoric reptile, is the most impressive of the monsters to come from Toho studios. Rodan was teamed with Godzilla and others in later movies.

Son of Kong (1933). Director, Ernest B. Schoedsack. Stars: Robert Armstrong, Helen Mack, Victor

Wong. A comic quickie made to cash in on the enormous success of *King Kong*. One of the original directors, some of the original cast, and Willis O'Brien worked on this.

Twenty Million Miles to Earth (1957). Director, Nathan Juran. Stars: William Hopper, Joan Taylor, Frank Puglia. A dinosaurlike creature from Venus lands on Earth and runs amok. Excellent Ray Harryhausen special effects.

The Valley of Gwangi (1969). Director, James O'Connolly. Stars: James Franciscus, Aila Golan, Richard Carlson. Wild West show captures a dinosaur living in a secret valley in Mexico. The plot is familiar, the Ray Harryhausen special effects are wonderful.

When Dinosaurs Ruled the Earth (1970, British). Director, Val Guest. Stars: Victoria Verti, Robin Hardon, Patrick Allen. Hammer studio's sequel to its own *One Million Years B.C.* Fine dinosaurs animated by Jim Danforth.

About the Author

DANIEL COHEN is the author of over a hundred books for both young readers and adults, and he is a former managing editor of *Science Digest* magazine. His titles include *Supermonsters, The Greatest Monsters in the World, Real Ghosts, Ghostly Terrors, Science Fiction's Greatest Monsters, The World's Most Famous Ghosts* and *Monsters You Never Heard Of,* all of which are available in Archway Paperback editions.

Mr. Cohen was born in Chicago and has a degree in journalism from the University of Illinois. He appears frequently on radio and television and has lectured at colleges and universities throughout the country. He lives with his wife, young daughter, one dog and four cats in Port Jervis, New York.

DRAGON MASTERS

WAKING THE RAINBOW DRAGON

BY

TRACEY WEST

ILLUSTRATED BY

DAMIEN JONES

SCHOLASTIC INC.

DRAGON MASTERS

Read All the Adventures

More books coming soon!

TABLE OF CONTENTS

FOR TRISTAN AND CORA,

who were chosen by the Dragon Stone. —TW

Text copyright © 2018 by Tracey West
Interior illustrations copyright © 2018 Scholastic Inc.

Library of Congress Cataloging-in-Publication Data
Names: West, Tracey, 1965- author. Jones, Damien, illustrator. West, Tracey, 1965- Dragon Masters; 10.
Title: Waking the rainbow dragon/by Tracey West; illustrated by Damien Jones.
Description: First edition. New York, NY: Branches/Scholastic Inc., 2018. Series: Dragon masters; 10
Summary: Drake has a dream about a new dragon that is somehow trapped in a cave, so Drake, Ana, and their two dragons set off to find the Rainbow Dragon's dragon master, Obi, and together they must rescue Rainbow dragon, Dayo, from Kwaku, a giant spider, who spins a deadly web.
Identifiers: LCCN 2017037057 ISBN 9789389823103 (pbk.) ISBN 9781338169904 (hardcover)
Subjects: LCSH: Dragons—Juvenile fiction. Magic—Juvenile fiction. Spiders—Juvenile fiction. Adventure stories. CYAC: Dragons—Fiction. Magic—Fiction. Spiders—Fiction. Adventure and adventurers—Fiction.
Classification: LCC PZ7.W51937 Wak 2018 DDC 813.54 [Fic] —dc23 LC record available at
https://lccn.loc.gov/2017037057

ISBN: 978-93-8982-310-3

First printing, July 2018
This edition, August 2021

Illustrated by Damien Jones
Edited by Katie Carella
Book design by Jessica Meltzer

Printed in India at Polykam Offset, Naraina, New Delhi - 110028

DRAKE'S DREAM

Drake was dreaming about a dragon.

Months before, Drake had been chosen to be a Dragon Master. He had been taken from his home and brought to King Roland's castle. There, he had learned that dragons were real.

Drake had been given his own dragon, Worm, a powerful Earth Dragon. Now they lived in the castle with the other Dragon Masters and their dragons: Kepri, a Sun Dragon; Shu, a Water Dragon; Vulcan, a Fire Dragon; and Zera, a Poison Dragon.

1

He had met other dragons during his adventures: Wati, a Moon Dragon; Lalo, a Lightning Dragon; Neru, a Thunder Dragon; and Frost, an Ice Dragon.

Drake dreamed about these dragons all the time. But the dragon in *this* dream was different.

She had a long body, like a snake's. Her scales shimmered with rows of stripes in different colors — red, orange, yellow, green, blue, and purple. Just like a rainbow.

It was a beautiful dream. The Rainbow Dragon flew across a blue sky. Her body curved like a rainbow. White clouds appeared and rain began to fall.

But then the rain stopped. The earth dried up. The scene changed to a dark cave. The Rainbow Dragon was curled up there. She looked frightened. A shadowy figure came toward her...

Drake jolted awake. His best friend, Bo, sat up across the room.

"Are you okay, Drake?" Bo asked.

"Yes," Drake replied. "I just had a dream. It felt so real. It was about a dragon."

"Are you sure it was a dream?" Bo asked. "Your Dragon Stone is glowing. Maybe Worm was trying to tell you something."

Drake looked down at the green stone that hung from a chain around his neck. Every Dragon Master wore one. It allowed them to connect with their dragons.

"You might be right, Bo!" Drake said. He jumped out of bed and quickly got dressed. "I'll find out! See you at breakfast!"

Drake ran downstairs. He raced through the underground Training Room to the caves where the dragons slept. He found Worm waiting for him.

"Worm, did you send me that dream? The dream about the Rainbow Dragon?" Drake asked.

Worm nodded. Drake's Dragon Stone glowed again. He heard Worm's voice inside his head.

Yes, Worm said. *The Rainbow Dragon needs our help!*

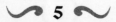

THE POWER OF RAIN

Where is the Rainbow Dragon?" Drake asked.

Worm shook his head. *I do not know.*

Drake frowned. "Griffith will know how to find her," he said.

Drake ran upstairs to the dining room. Griffith, the wizard who taught them, was there. He was eating breakfast with the other Dragon Masters who lived in the castle: Bo, Rori, Ana, and Petra.

"I told the others that Worm sent you a dream," Bo said when Drake came in.

"It was about a Rainbow Dragon," Drake explained. "Worm says she's in trouble. But that's all he knows."

Griffith nodded. "Very interesting," he said. "There is a legend about a Rainbow Dragon. She is the only one of her kind. She is very old, and very powerful. My guess is that this dragon must be sending messages to Worm somehow."

"Do you know where she lives?" Drake asked.

"I can't recall," Griffith said. "But I am sure we'll find information in one of our books. Let's get to the classroom!"

Drake wolfed down an apple, a hunk of cheese, and a piece of bread. Then the wizard and five Dragon Masters walked to the lowest level of the castle.

"What did the Rainbow Dragon look like in your dream?" Ana asked. Her dark eyes shone. "Was she beautiful?"

Drake nodded. "Yes. She had shimmering scales in rainbow colors."

"Big deal," said red-haired Rori. "What kinds of powers could a Rainbow Dragon have? Does she shoot color beams? She can't be as powerful as a Fire Dragon, like Vulcan."

"Maybe she has special powers," Petra said. "After all, Worm looks plain. But he is the most powerful dragon we know."

Rori frowned. Drake knew she couldn't argue with that. Worm could move or break things with the power of his mind. He could transport himself and others anywhere in the world in a flash.

They reached the classroom. Griffith started taking books off a shelf and handing them out.

The room was quiet as the Dragon Masters flipped through the pages.

Bo broke the silence. "I found something!" he cried. "Here is a story about a Rainbow Dragon that lives in the Kingdom of Ifri."

"Is that far from where we are, in the Kingdom of Bracken?" Petra asked.

"I know where Ifri is!" Ana said. She ran to a shelf. She came back and unrolled a map on the table.

"This is the Land of Pyramids, where I am from," she said. "And over here is the Kingdom of Ifri. It is a long way from my home, but my father has traveled there."

"What else does the story say?" Petra asked.

Bo read aloud, "The Rainbow Dragon has the powers of rain. Every year she comes out of her cave and brings rain to the land."

"Just like in my dream!" Drake said. "But then I saw her in her cave. She looked . . . trapped. And something was coming after her!"

"If the Rainbow Dragon is trapped, then she can't make rain," Rori said.

Ana gasped. "Oh no!" she cried. "Without rain, plants will die. There will be no food."

"I'm afraid you're right," Griffith agreed. "Ifri is in real trouble!"

A NEW DRAGON MASTER?

We've got to help the Rainbow Dragon!" Drake said. "We need to go to Ifri!"

"Ifri is very big," Ana said, pointing at the map. "How will we find the dragon?"

Drake shrugged. "Worm doesn't know where she is. So he can't transport us to her cave."

Petra looked at Griffith. "Can you use magic to find the Rainbow Dragon?"

Griffith stroked his long, white beard. "I can try."

Everyone followed the wizard to his workshop. He walked to a small table and took a cloth off a gazing ball. He bent over the glass globe and waved his hand over it.

The Dragon Masters watched the ball. A cloud of smoke swirled inside it.

Griffith frowned. "I cannot see anything," he said. "There is some kind of magic hiding the Rainbow Dragon."

Bo looked down at his Dragon Stone. "Does the Rainbow Dragon have a Dragon Master?" he asked.

"Excellent question, Bo!" Griffith said. "If we can find the Dragon Master, then maybe we can find the Rainbow Dragon."

He hurried over to a wooden box and opened it. Inside glittered a large, green stone — the Dragon Stone. Each Dragon Master's stone came from it.

"Dragon Stone, show me the Dragon Master of the Rainbow Dragon," Griffith asked.

Bright green light shot out of the stone. Moving pictures appeared inside the light.

A boy stood in front of a well. He pulled up a bucket and frowned. The well should have had water in it. But the bucket was empty. He showed it to a woman nearby.

"The well is dry," she told him. "It is like this all over Ifri."

Then the green light faded.

"Is that boy the Dragon Master?" Rori asked.

Griffith nodded. "Yes. He is the true Dragon Master chosen by the Dragon Stone," he said. "And this discovery brings us one step closer to finding the Rainbow Dragon."

The wizard clapped. "We must travel to Ifri and find this boy at once!"

CHAPTER 4

A STRANGE MESSAGE

"W orm can transport us to Ifri," Drake pointed out. "But how will we find the new Dragon Master once we land? The boy could be anywhere in Ifri."

"I have been working on a spell that can locate Dragon Masters," Griffith said. "I will get that ready. Drake and Ana, prepare your dragons for the journey. You two will come with me."

"Just Drake and Ana? What about the rest of us?" Rori asked.

"You must stay behind, to protect the castle," Griffith said.

Rori nodded. "Bo, Petra, and I will make sure nothing bad happens here while you're gone."

As she spoke, a sparkling blue bubble floated into Griffith's workshop.

"Look!" Petra cried.

POP! The bubble burst right in front of Griffith. A piece of paper fell into his hands. He opened it up.

"What does it say?" Ana asked.

"It is a message from the Wizard's Council," Griffith replied. Then his face went dark. "Drake, Ana, I am afraid I cannot go with you. I must deal with this message. But I trust that you will find the Rainbow Dragon. If you need help, transport back here right away."

Drake and Ana ran to the dragon caves and quickly returned to the Training Room with Worm and Kepri. Ana had put a saddle on Kepri's back.

They found Griffith looking down at the
map of Ifri with Bo and Rori.

"One moment," Griffith said. "I'm putting
the final spell on this map."

Griffith pointed at the map. Sparks flew
from his finger.

"Map, help Drake and Ana roam. To the
Dragon Master's home!" he rhymed.

The map glowed, and then it faded.

Griffith handed the map to Ana.

"This should show you the way once you land in Ifri," Griffith said. He opened a box and pulled out a Dragon Stone that dangled from a chain. He handed it to Drake. "Give this to the new Dragon Master when you see him."

Drake nodded. "Yes, Griffith." He tucked the stone into his pocket.

Petra ran up to them, out of breath.

"Wait!" she cried. She had a small bag in each hand. She gave one to Drake, and one to Ana. "I collected some food for your journey. And water."

"Thanks," Drake said, and Ana hugged Petra.

Then Ana touched Kepri with one hand, and Worm with the other. Drake touched Worm.

"Good luck!" Bo said.

"Hurry back!" Rori added.

Drake looked up at Worm. "Take us to the Land of Ifri!" he said.

Worm's body began to glow green. A bright, green light exploded in the Training Room.

Drake blinked. His body felt tingly. The green light faded, and he saw a blue sky and bright sun above his head.

"We're here!" Ana cheered.

Drake looked around. The land was very flat for as far as he could see. The tall grass was turning yellow. Some short trees popped up here and there, but their leaves were dying. There was no sign of a village.

"Which way should we go?" Drake asked.

Ana unrolled the map. A blue, glowing line appeared.

"Let's follow the magic map!" she said.

CHAPTER 5

FOLLOW THE MAP

Ana and Drake walked across the grassy land. Kepri walked behind Ana, and Worm slithered behind Drake.

The hot sun shone overhead as they walked. Colorful birds flew from tree to tree.

"Most of the birds in Bracken are brown. Or gray," Drake said.

"Ifri is full of many creatures you won't find in Bracken," Ana told him.

"I hope we see more," Drake said. "But mostly, I want to find the Dragon Master!"

They walked and walked, following the map.

"My father said there are many beautiful waterfalls in Ifri," Ana remarked. "But we haven't seen any yet."

"*Everything* looks dried up," Drake said, looking at the yellow grass beneath his feet. "How much farther?"

"I don't know," she replied. "The map doesn't show where we're supposed to stop. The blue line just keeps getting longer as we walk."

Drake looked at the setting sun.

"It's getting late," he said.

"We can sleep under the stars," Ana said. "I've done it before, when I traveled with my father. Don't worry. I'll find us a good spot."

Ana soon found a spot inside a circle of trees. They both sat down in the grass.

"We'll camp here for the night," Ana said.

Drake nodded. "It feels good to rest." He opened the bag Petra had given him and took out a pouch filled with water. "And I'm so thirsty!"

He took a drink.

"Can I see the map?" Drake asked.

"Sure," Ana said. "There's just a blue dot on it now, since we've stopped."

Drake took the map from Ana. "There's got to be something here that shows us where the new Dragon Master's village is," he said. He took another sip of water — and the pouch slipped from his hand! Water spilled onto the map. The black ink faded. The blue dot disappeared.

"Drake!" Ana yelled. "What did you do?"

"It was an accident!" Drake yelled back.

"I know." Ana paused. "I'm sorry I yelled. But the spell is ruined."

Drake took a deep breath. He didn't want to fail Griffith. They had to rescue the Rainbow Dragon and save Ifri.

"Let's get some rest," he said. "We're both tired. Maybe the map will dry out overnight."

"I hope you're right," Ana said, yawning. "We'll check it in the morning."

The two Dragon Masters ate some apples and bread. The night air was chilly, so Worm curled his body around Drake. Ana snuggled against Kepri. They slept soundly.

When Drake opened his eyes, four enormous creatures surrounded their camp!

WILD FRIENDS

"Ana, wake up!" Drake yelled. "We're surrounded by dragons! Well — I *think* they're dragons!"

The four creatures were as big as dragons. But they had very long, skinny noses. They had gray, wrinkly skin instead of scales. Their big ears looked like wings to Drake.

Ana laughed. "They're not dragons, Drake," she said. "They're called elephants. And they're friendly. Well, usually they are."

Worm studied the elephants. Then his eyes began to glow. The elephants made trumpeting sounds with their trunks and shuffled their feet.

Drake's Dragon Stone glowed. He heard Worm's voice inside his head.

"Worm asked the elephants to help us. They know of a village not far from here," Drake told Ana. "They will lead us part of the way."

Ana looked down at the map. "That's a good thing, because the map still isn't working."

"Elephants to the rescue!" Drake said.

Drake and Ana ate breakfast. Then they followed the slow-moving elephants across the land. After a short time, they stopped at a shallow pool of water in the ground. The elephants sucked up the water in their long noses and then brought the water to their mouths. Worm and Kepri drank, too.

The elephants waved their trunks at Worm and walked away. Drake heard words inside his head.

The elephants told me how to get to the village. Follow me.

Drake motioned for Ana and Kepri to follow Worm.

"What about the Rainbow Dragon?" Drake asked Worm as they walked on. "Can you still feel her energy?"

It is weak, Worm replied. *Something keeps blocking my mind powers. I feel her, but her location is ... fuzzy.*

Just then, Ana cried, "Drake! Look! It's the village!"

Drake turned and saw a bunch of round houses with pointy tops. Lots of people were walking around.

Then Drake spotted the boy that the Dragon Stone had shown them.

"There he is!" Drake yelled. "It's the new Dragon Master!"

CHAPTER 7

THE CHOSEN ONE

Drake and Ana ran over to the new Dragon Master. The boy looked up at Worm and Kepri. His eyes got wide.

All the villagers began staring at the dragons. No one ran or started screaming. They actually moved closer.

"Are those . . . dragons?" the boy asked. "We have many legends about dragons here. But we have never seen any."

Drake nodded. "Yes, they are dragons," he said. "I'm Drake, and this is my dragon, Worm."

"And I'm Ana. My dragon's name is Kepri," Ana said with a smile.

"I am Obi," the boy said. "Welcome to our village. What brings you here?"

"We came to find *you*," Drake said. "You need to help the Rainbow Dragon."

Obi's mouth dropped open. The villagers all began to talk at once. A man and a woman walked up behind Obi.

"We are Obi's parents," the man said. "Please tell us where you are from, and what you know about the Rainbow Dragon."

"We came from the Kingdom of Bracken in the north," Ana replied.

Drake patted Worm's neck. "My dragon got a message from the Rainbow Dragon. She told Worm that she is in trouble."

Obi's parents looked at each other.

"This is what we have feared," Obi's father said. "The rains have not come. Water is hard to find. Plants are dying. We will soon run out of food."

"But how can Obi help?" Obi's mother asked.

"Our wizard has a Dragon Stone," Drake said. "It showed us that Obi has a special connection with the Rainbow Dragon. He is her Dragon Master. He may be the only one who can help her."

Obi shook his head. "That makes no sense," he said. "The Rainbow Dragon does not need a master. She is very powerful."

"Even the most powerful dragons need help sometimes," Ana said. "Do you know where she might be?"

Obi shook his head. "The legend says she lives in a cave somewhere," he replied. "She has never been seen. But when the rains come and a rainbow appears, we know that she has helped us."

Drake took the piece of the Dragon Stone from his pocket. "You are her Dragon Master. You can use your connection with her to help us find her."

Obi's father spoke up. "It is our good fortune that these visitors came here. You must help them, Obi."

"How can *I* help?" Obi asked. "I am just a boy. Someone else should go. A warrior. Or a healer. Or a teacher."

Ana took the Dragon Stone from Drake and put it around Obi's neck.

"The Dragon Stone picked you," she said. "You are the chosen one."

Obi looked at his parents. He looked down at the stone. Then he took a deep breath.

"All right," he said. "I will help you!"

"Yes!" Ana cheered.

"But I do not know how to find the Rainbow Dragon," Obi said.

"Worm is getting some fuzzy energy signals from the Rainbow Dragon," Drake explained. "He can lead us in the right direction."

"Then your link with the Rainbow Dragon will take us the rest of the way," Ana said. "Your Dragon Stone will glow green when you connect with her. She will lead you to her."

Obi's mother kissed her son on the head. "Be safe. The village is counting on you."

The villagers waved as Obi left with Drake, Ana, and the dragons.

THE JOURNEY

The Dragon Masters and the dragons made their way across the grassland.

"What is your kingdom like?" Obi asked as they walked.

"Well, Bracken is not flat like here," Drake replied. "There are mountains."

"And there are a lot more trees," Ana added.

"I used to live on a farm," Drake told Obi. "One year, we had a summer with very little rain. A lot of the crops died. It was scary."

Obi nodded. "Without our crops, there will be no food to eat."

Drake picked up his water pouch and frowned. "Rats. I'm almost out of water."

"Me, too," Ana added.

"I think there is a watering hole around here," Obi said. He walked ahead of Ana and Drake, looking at the ground. Then he broke away from the path.

"Where are you going?" Drake asked. He and Ana hurried to catch up to Obi.

"These are animal tracks," Obi explained, pointing to the ground. "And they lead right ... here."

He pushed through some bushes, and they stepped into a clearing. A small pool of water bubbled up from the dirt.

"Wow!" Drake cried.

"You found water!" Ana said happily.

They filled their pouches with water. Worm took a drink, too.

Then Obi led them back through the bushes.

Suddenly, Obi froze. He stopped Drake with his arm.

A strange animal stood in the grass ahead of them. It looked like a very big, very hairy pig with long, white tusks!

The animal's ears twitched. Then it turned around and locked eyes with Drake.

KWAKU!

Obi put a finger to his lips. "*Shh!* Don't move," he whispered to Drake and Ana. "It's a warthog! If you make any fast movements, it might attack."

Obi raised his arms above his head and crept up to the warthog. Then he made a very loud, scary noise.

ROOOAAAAAR!

Frightened, the warthog squealed and scrambled away.

"Wow, Obi! That was awesome!" Drake said. "You sounded like a big, scary cat."

"I was pretending to be a lion," Obi said. "Do you have lions in Bracken?"

Drake shook his head.

"They are big, fierce cats," Obi explained.

Ana smiled at Obi. "You are very smart and brave. I think you were born to be a Dragon Master."

"Yes," Drake agreed. "You found water for us. You scared away the warty hog. You're amazing!"

Obi gave them both a shy smile. They caught up to Worm and Kepri, who had started moving again.

A few minutes later, Obi's Dragon Stone began to glow faintly.

"Obi, look!" Drake cried, pointing. "Your stone is glowing. The Rainbow Dragon is trying to connect with you."

Worm stopped.

Obi must lead us the rest of the way, he told Drake. *His connection is stronger than mine.*

"Worm says you should lead us," Drake told Obi.

"How do I do that?" Obi asked.

"Can you feel the pull of your dragon's energy?" Ana said.

Obi closed his eyes. "It's weak, but I can feel it!" he said, his voice rising with excitement. "It's like ... she's in my head."

"Great! Now walk toward that energy," Ana instructed.

Obi started walking. They followed him to a low hill. A big hole in the hill led to an underground tunnel.

Obi gazed into the tunnel. "I . . . I think she is in here," he said.

Ana looked up at Kepri. "Can you please light the way for us?"

A white ball of light floated out of Kepri's mouth. It hung in the air, lighting up the dark tunnel.

The ball floated down the tunnel, and the others followed it.

They went a short way and then stopped.
A thick spiderweb blocked the entrance to a
cave!

"Whoa! A *very* big spider must have made
this," Drake said.

Obi gasped. "Kwaku!" he cried.

"What's a kwaku?" Drake asked.

"Kwaku is a giant spider that my people tell stories about," Obi explained. "Sometimes he is a hero. Sometimes he makes trouble."

"Are they true stories?" Drake asked.

"I thought they were just legends," Obi said. "But look at this web! Only Kwaku could have spun it."

Suddenly, Drake's Dragon Stone began to glow. He heard Worm's voice inside his head.

Obi is right. Kwaku has trapped the Rainbow Dragon inside her cave!

STUCK IN A WEB

Drake ran to the giant web blocking the entrance to the cave. He started pulling on the strands.

"I can't break the web!" he said. "It is too strong and sticky!"

"Drake, stop!" Ana said. "If there is a giant spider behind there, we need a plan."

She turned to Obi. "In the stories about Kwaku, how is he defeated?" she asked.

"I don't think he has ever been beaten. Kwaku is a magical trickster. He usually uses tricks to escape," Obi said.

"There must be a way to stop him," Drake said.

"Well, some stories say he works for the ruler of the sun. So maybe the sun can stop Kwaku?" Obi guessed.

"Hmm," Ana said. "Kepri might not be the ruler of the sun. But she has the powers of the sun! Maybe she can break through the web and fight Kwaku's magic."

Ana turned to Kepri. "Use a sunbeam on the web!"

Kepri opened her mouth and shot a strong beam of sunlight at the thick spiderweb. The strands of the web began to shimmer. Then they disappeared!

"It worked!" Drake cried.

Obi put a finger to his lips. "Quiet."

They stepped into the cave. The ball of white sunlight still floated in the air, lighting the dark space.

Drake and Ana gasped.

A dragon with a very long body was wrapped in a cocoon of spider silk. Through the silk, Drake could see the dragon's rainbow-colored scales.

"The Rainbow Dragon!" Obi cried.

"Kepri, use another sunbeam to get rid of the cocoon!" Ana commanded.

The Sun Dragon aimed a strong beam of sunlight at the Rainbow Dragon. The webs began to shimmer, but before they could disappear...

Click, click, click! A loud, clicking sound began to echo through the cave. Kepri stopped shooting her sunbeam and turned toward the sound.

A giant spider crawled out of the shadows! His eight long legs were black with yellow stripes. His round body had a black-and-yellow pattern. Eight round, black eyes stared at the Dragon Masters and their dragons. Drake, Ana, and Obi started to slowly back up.

Eeeeeeeee! With a cry, the spider scurried toward them. Kepri and Worm charged forward, protecting the Dragon Masters.

"Kepri, hit him with sunlight!" Ana yelled.

Kepri aimed a beam of sunlight at Kwaku. The spider jumped up to avoid it. He hung upside down from the ceiling of the cave.

In a flash, he shot webs at Kepri.

The webs wrapped around her mouth. Kepri couldn't fight back. The webs magically grew and twisted all around Kepri's body.

"Kepri!" Ana cried.

Worm's body began to glow green. But before he could use his powers, Kwaku hit him with webs, too. The webs wrapped around Worm. Within seconds, he was trapped inside a cocoon.

"Quick, hide!" Drake yelled to Ana and Obi. "We can't help the dragons if Kwaku gets us, too!"

The friends raced behind a big rock. Drake touched his Dragon Stone.

"Worm, can you hear me?" he whispered.

Drake's Dragon Stone glowed faintly. Drake heard a muffled voice in his head.

He turned to Ana and Obi. "Worm is trying to tell me something, but I can't understand him," he said. "The cocoon must be blocking Worm's powers!"

"I can't hear Kepri's voice in my head, either," Ana whispered.

"What now?" Drake asked. "We can't fight Kwaku without our dragons!"

A STRONG CONNECTION

rake, Ana, and Obi stayed hidden behind the rock. But the clicking sound of the giant spider grew louder as he got closer.

Click, click, click.

"We should go get help," Obi whispered.

"Who will help us?" Drake asked.

Click, click, click.

"We can't stay here," Ana said. "Kwaku is going to trap us in cocoons, too!"

Obi stood up. His Dragon Stone was glowing.

"Obi, get down!" Drake hissed.

Obi didn't listen to Drake. He stared at the Rainbow Dragon.

Kwaku spotted Obi with one of his eight eyes.

"Watch out, Obi! Kwaku will hit you with one of his webs!" Drake yelled.

Obi didn't run. He talked to the Rainbow Dragon.

"Our village needs you," he said. "Please help us."

Then Obi's Dragon Stone began to glow brighter . . . and brighter . . . and brighter!

"Whoa!" Drake told Ana. "I've never seen a Dragon Stone glow like that before. It's even brighter than Worm when he uses his powers!"

The bright green light filled the cave. The Dragon Masters had to shield their eyes.

Eeeeeeeeeeeeeeeee! Kwaku shrieked.

As the powerful light grew, he skittered deep into the cave.

The light faded. Drake looked around. The cocoons around the dragons were shimmering, just like when Kepri's sunlight hit the giant web.

The cocoons disappeared. Drake and Ana
ran to their dragons.

Ana patted Kepri's head.

"Worm! Are you okay?" Drake asked.

I am fine, Worm replied.

Drake smiled and glanced over at Obi.

The new Dragon Master was standing
next to the Rainbow Dragon. She was free of
the cocoon, and hovering above the floor.

"She's so beautiful," Ana whispered.

The Rainbow Dragon's colorful scales shimmered in the dim light of the cave. She had a long, snakelike body like Worm's. She did not have wings.

Obi turned to Drake and Ana. "She says it's time to make it rain. And she wants me to go with her."

Drake nodded.

Obi climbed onto the Rainbow Dragon's back. Then they floated out of the cave, past Drake, Ana, and their dragons.

Ana nudged Drake. "Let's go!"

They ran outside, followed by Worm and Kepri. The sun shone brightly in the blue sky.

The Rainbow Dragon flew up, up above the grassy lands, with Obi on her back.

"I'll meet you back at the village!" Obi called down.

Obi and the dragon flew higher and higher. Gray clouds appeared in the sky.

Then Drake felt one cold, wet drop on his cheek.

"Rain!" he cheered.

DRAGONS IN THE SKY

More clouds filled the sky. The rain began to fall harder.

"Obi will be busy for a while," Drake said. "Let's go tell his parents what happened."

Ana nodded. She touched Kepri with one hand and Worm with the other.

Worm transported them to the village in a flash of green light. They found the villagers standing outside in the rain.

Obi's parents ran up to them.

"Where is Obi?" Obi's mother asked.

"He is safe!" Drake replied. "Kwaku the spider was keeping the Rainbow Dragon prisoner. Obi freed her. They are both up in the sky now, making rain."

Obi's mother took Ana by the hand. "Come, both of you. I think this will be a long rain. Step inside our hut, where it is warm and dry."

Obi's mother fed them bowls of hot stew.

Just as they were finishing, a shout came from outside the hut.

"Look!"

Drake, Ana, and Obi's parents rushed outside.

The clouds were floating away. The sun was shining. The sky was bright blue. And the Rainbow Dragon was floating in the sky. Her body curved, just like a rainbow. Her colorful scales shimmered brightly. Obi sat on her back, beaming happily.

Everyone stared at the

Th
She s
"K
A
up
ai
m

en Ana's Dragon Stone began to glow.
miled.

Kepri wants to fly, too," she said.

Ana climbed onto Kepri's back. Kepri flew into the sky. Misty waterdrops filled the
. She shot a beam of sunlight from her
outh. The light hit the water droplets and
made a rainbow right underneath the
Rainbow Dragon.

Drake grinned. "It's a double rainbow!"

DAYO'S STORY

Kepri and the Rainbow Dragon flew down from the sky. Obi slid off the Rainbow Dragon's back and ran to his parents.

"Mom! Dad!" he cried.

"Hooray for Obi!" the villagers cheered.

Obi's Dragon Stone began to glow.

"The Rainbow Dragon wants me to tell you her story," he said. "Her name is Dayo."

"Dayo," Ana repeated, hopping off Kepri. "That's a cool name!"

"Did she say how Kwaku trapped her in her cave?" Drake asked.

"Kwaku tricked her," Obi went on. "He told the Rainbow Dragon he knew the most beautiful song in the world. She asked to hear it. But the song was really a spell that made her fall asleep. Then he spun a cocoon around her."

Some of the villagers gasped.

"Why would he do that?" Ana asked.

"Kwaku was mad at Dayo," Obi explained. "The last time the rains came, water flooded his den. He trapped Dayo because he didn't want that to happen ever again."

Obi's father nodded. "He is a tricky one!" he said.

"Dayo couldn't move, but her mind was still powerful," Obi continued. "She called out for help. And Drake's dragon, Worm, heard her."

Drake patted Worm. "And then Worm told me," he said. "And then we found Obi."

"Dayo is grateful to you both, and your dragons," Obi told Drake and Ana.

Two young boys ran into the village.

"The waterfall is flowing again!" one of them shouted.

The villagers cheered and hugged one another.

"I'm glad the Rainbow Dragon is safe now," Ana said. "But what if Kwaku tries to trick her again?"

"Dayo says she knows not to trust Kwaku ever again," Obi replied. "And now that she and I have connected, she will call on me if she is in trouble."

Obi looked down at his glowing Dragon Stone. A sad look crossed his face.

"Dayo says that she must go back to her cave," he said. "She must watch over the land, like she always has."

He hugged his dragon. "I will miss you, Dayo," he said.

The Rainbow Dragon wrapped her body around Obi, giving him a quick hug.

Then she floated up into the sky and flew away.

"I was hoping that you and Dayo could come back to Bracken and train with us," Drake said.

"We cannot, but thank you," Obi said. "The Rainbow Dragon belongs in this land. And so do I."

"I understand," Drake replied.

Obi's father stepped forward. "Thank you for helping our village," he said. "You will always be welcome here."

"Thank you," Drake said. "Now we must get home. Our friends will be getting worried about us."

"Good-bye!" Ana called out.

Drake and Ana touched their dragons. Then Worm transported the four of them back to Bracken in a flash of green light.

TROUBLE AT THE CASTLE

"Diego, what are you doing?!"

The first thing Drake and Ana heard when they landed in the Training Room was Griffith's voice. He sounded angry. They quickly left Worm and Kepri and followed the sound to the classroom.

"Please stop!" Griffith was yelling at a short, round wizard. Diego was Griffith's friend, and he had helped the Dragon Masters many times. But now he was making a mess of the classroom. He took book after book off the shelf and tossed each one on the floor.

"Where is it? It has got to be here!" Diego muttered to himself. He ignored Griffith.

"Diego, calm down!" Griffith ordered.

Suddenly Diego held up a book. "I found it!" he cried. He spun around, facing Griffith.

Griffith gasped. His mouth dropped open in surprise.

That's when Drake noticed something — Diego's eyes were red!

"Diego! Let us help you!" Drake cried, but Diego had a special talent. He could transport, just like Worm.

Poof! The wizard disappeared.

Rori, Bo, and Petra came running into the classroom.

"What's all the yelling about?" Rori asked. Then she stopped. "Drake! Ana! You're back!"

"Yes, and we saved the Rainbow Dragon," Ana said. "But that's not why Griffith was yelling. Diego was just here!"

"His eyes were red — the color of Maldred's dark magic," Drake said. "I think he was under a spell!"

Everyone was quiet. Maldred was an evil wizard. He had attacked King Roland's castle and tried to take the dragons away. The Dragon Masters, Griffith, and Diego had stopped him.

Bo turned to Griffith. "But you and Diego sent Maldred to the Wizard's Council Prison," he said. "He can't use magic while he's in there."

"That is what the council warned me about earlier..." the wizard replied. "Maldred has escaped."

"No!" Rori yelled. She balled her hands into fists. "We need to find him!"

"What would he want with Diego?" Petra asked.

"It looks like Maldred has used Diego to steal a book from me," Griffith said as he riffled through the bookshelf. "But — no, wait, it couldn't be . . ." His face turned pale. "Diego took my book about the Naga, a dragon of legend."

"Is that bad?" Drake asked.

Griffith nodded. "Very bad. If Maldred is seeking the Naga, then the whole world is in danger!"

TRACEY WEST was once lucky enough to see a double rainbow, and she hopes you'll get to see one, too.

Tracey has written dozens of books for kids. She writes in the house she shares with her husband, her three stepkids (when they're home from college), and her animal friends. She has three dogs and one cat, who sits on her desk when she writes! Thankfully, the cat does not weigh as much as a dragon.

DAMIEN JONES lives with his wife and son in Cornwall — the home of the legend of King Arthur. Cornwall even has its very own castle! On clear days you can see for miles from the top of the castle, making it the perfect lookout for dragons.

Damien has illustrated children's books. He has also animated films and television programs. He works in a studio surrounded by figures of mystical characters that keep an eye on him as he draws.

DRAGON MASTERS
WAKING THE RAINBOW DRAGON

Questions and Activities

Drake has a dream at the beginning of the story. Who sends him the dream? Why?

Why is the Rainbow Dragon important to the Kingdom of Ifri? Turn back to pages 11 and 36.

How did Kwaku trick the Rainbow Dragon? (Hint! Look back on page 79.)

At the end of the story, the Dragon Masters discover that Diego is under Maldred's spell. What do you think the dark wizard wants with Diego? Predict what will happen in the next book. Write your own beginning chapter, and draw your own action-packed pictures.

Drake and Ana see elephants and a warthog in the Kingdom of Ifri. What wild animal would you most like to see in real life? Where does this animal live? Using nonfiction books and the Internet, learn more about this animal.